THE

Born in 1968, Fabrice Bourland lives in Paris. He has worked extensively as a book and magazine editor, and many of his own short stories have been published in French. *The Baker Street Phantom* is his first fantasy crime novel.

Morag Young studied French and Italian at Leeds University and subsequently worked for the European institutions in Brussels and Strasbourg. She lives in Kent and works as a translator.

THE BAKER STREET
PHANTOM

THE BAKER STREET PHANTOM

FABRICE BOURLAND

Translated by Morag Young

GALLIC BOOKS
London

A Gallic Book

First published in France as *Le fantôme de Baker Street* by Éditions 10/18

Copyright © Éditions 10/18, Département d'Univers Poche, 2008
English translation copyright © Gallic Books 2010

First published in Great Britain in 2010 by Gallic Books, 134 Lots Road,
London SW10 0RJ

This book is copyright under the Berne Convention
No reproduction without permission
All rights reserved

A CIP record for this book is available from the British Library

ISBN 978-1-906040-28-4

Typeset in Fournier MT by SX Composing DTP, Rayleigh, Essex

Printed and bound by CPI Bookmarque, Croydon, CR0 4TD

2 4 6 8 10 9 7 5 3 1

To Véronique, Félix and Rosalie

CONTENTS

Foreword by the Publisher   xv

I   Extract from an Article in the *Toronto
        Daily News*, 26 July 1932   1
II   A Most Unexpected Visit   9
III   Introducing James Trelawney and Your Narrator   13
IV   A Most Unexpected Visit (Continued)   21
V   Another Murder in London   29
VI   A Visit to 221 Baker Street   37
VII   More Crimes in the East End   49
VIII   A Surprising Spiritualist Séance   57
IX   James Reviews the Case   73
X   A Little Reading Never Hurt Anyone   87
XI   A Night in the East End   97
XII   We Learn Why and How   110
XIII   Return to Baker Street   123
XIV   A Few Hours' Well-Deserved Rest   141
XV   The Search for the Piccadilly House   147
XVI   At Highgate Cemetery   157

Epilogue   174
Note to the Reader   180
Notes   182

'If I don't kill him soon, he'll kill me.'
Sir Arthur Conan Doyle to Silas Hocking in the summer of
1893, reported in *New Age* magazine in 1895

'He must go the way of all flesh, material or imaginary.
One likes to think that there is some fantastic limbo for the
children of the imagination, some strange, impossible place
where the beaux of Fielding may still make love to the belles
of Richardson, where Scott's heroes still may strut, Dickens's
delightful Cockneys still raise a laugh, and Thackeray's
worldlings continue to carry on their reprehensible careers.'
Sir Arthur Conan Doyle
Preface to the original edition of *The Case-Book of Sherlock
Holmes*, 1927

'There was a small doctor dwelling near me, small in
stature and also, I fear, in practice, whom I will call Brown. He
was a student of the occult . . . From what I learned I should
judge that the powers of the society to which he belonged
included that of loosening their own etheric bodies, in
summoning the etheric bodies of others (mine, for example)
and in making thought images . . . But their line of philosophy
or development is beyond me. I believe they represent a
branch of Rosicrucians.'
Sir Arthur Conan Doyle, *Memories and Adventures*, 1924

FOREWORD BY THE PUBLISHER

I received the incredible story you are about to read in the post a few weeks ago. The manuscript came with a letter written on the elegant ivory notepaper of a legal practice in Northampton. In the letter William Barnett, a partner at Barnett & Hartmann, told us that he was the son of John W. Barnett, a solicitor who had died in March the previous year at the age of ninety-one. We were of course familiar with John Barnett who for many years had been the executor of Andrew Fowler Singleton, the famous detective and author who died in April 1972. Our publishing house had dealt with him several times in that capacity.

William Barnett told us that he had recently been going through his father's affairs. In the attic of the vast family home, he had discovered a suitcase containing an impressive collection of papers and notes of all kinds, some of sentimental value only, and a number of carefully arranged folders. The first, of a faded green, was captivatingly entitled 'The Baker Street Phantom'. Inside was a manuscript of two hundred typed sheets, which, at first glance, bore all the hallmarks of a new investigation by Mr Singleton.

The find immediately raised unanswerable questions: why had his father let the manuscript lie rotting at the bottom of a suitcase when, immediately after Andrew's death, he had been involved in distributing his unpublished work? Was it an unfortunate oversight or had he deliberately chosen to let it sink into oblivion? In other words, was its authenticity in doubt?

William had immediately immersed himself in the text and admitted in his letter to us that he had never read anything so disconcerting in his life.

Believing that he was neither sufficiently familiar with Andrew Singleton's work nor adequately au fait *with the science of spiritualism to determine the credibility of what he had read, William decided to send us the extraordinary manuscript on the basis that, since its creation, our illustrious house had published a number of the author's cases. He would leave us to judge whether it should be published or not.*

I have to admit that the <u>decision to publish</u> was not taken lightly. What was the story really? A tale retrospectively telling the first adventures of one of the best and most endearing amateur detectives of the twentieth century? If that were the case, and if it were true that events had occurred as described, we would find ourselves faced with a phenomenon with unimaginable consequences, which would resurrect ancient beliefs in the creative power of the imagination and make us consider the monsters created in the brains of our authors in a different light. Perhaps, however, it was pure fiction, deliberately unrealistic and unlikely, entirely invented by the author to give himself the opportunity to express himself more freely and candidly? As we read it, the most surprising aspect of those arresting pages was that Andrew Fowler Singleton chose to dwell on himself, his past, his childhood and his first encounter with his faithful associate, something he had never done in the rest of his work.

If it were established that this enlightening tale was just a product of his imagination, it would be unique in the author's work. It has been proved on a number of occasions (to the satisfaction of all, we hope) that both the traditional cases he pursued, which were limited to tangible reality, and the numerous affairs which led him to the edge of human logic and reason were all actually investigated by Andrew Singleton himself.

Unlike Arthur Conan Doyle, one of his literary heroes, Singleton really was a sleuth. We know that the illustrious British author, in a desire to right wrongs, successfully took on the case of George Edalji (found guilty in 1903 of killing livestock at several farms in Staffordshire) and the case of Oscar Slater (sentenced to life imprisonment in 1909 for murdering his landlady). In each case, having struggled to establish the truth, Conan Doyle managed to have the verdicts overturned and the two prisoners released. But those cases had none of the complexity and ingenuity of those devised by the creator of Sherlock Holmes in his stories. Moreover, later attempts to help the police find an anonymous individual in 1921 and Agatha Christie in 1926, when she mysteriously disappeared one evening in December and was not heard of for eleven days, ended in bitter failure. In both cases, with the help of a medium, Horace Leaf, Conan Doyle had attempted to put into practice the psychometric technique used in some of his fantastic tales: diagnosing the circumstances of the tragedy with varying degrees of precision by allowing the medium to touch an object which had belonged to the person who had disappeared.

As regards our manuscript, clearly deception remains a possibility. The style could easily be that of the detective but, it might be argued, what could be easier than imitating a style of writing? On the other hand, absolutely nothing in the events in question or their chronology indicates that there was any cheating. Of course, it will be pointed out that it is difficult to check whether the article in the Toronto Daily News, dated 26 July 1932, was invented by the author as the paper's archives were all destroyed in a fire in 1947. However (and we have checked ourselves), accounts of the Hamilton group's spiritualist meetings are easily accessible.

Nonetheless, even if the authenticity of the document is recognised, many aspects of the manuscript remain unclear. In particular, it appears to be impossible to determine with precision the date it was written. If we exclude the idea that it was written just after the events related (mention is made in the last lines of the manuscript of the death of Jean Leckie in 1940 and, earlier on, the death of James Trelawney, the faithful associate, killed by the Nazis a few weeks before their surrender), there is nothing to indicate whether it was written in the 1950s or 1960s, say, or whether it was written later still, during the last months of the author's life when he was enjoying his well-deserved retirement at his cottage near Halifax in Nova Scotia, dedicating his days and nights to his two favourite activities: reading and writing.

The fact remains that, after much reflection on the part of all of our directors, we finally agreed that it was important to make this story public.

We trust that we have taken the right decision. Now it is for others to decide.

Stanley Cartwright, 23 March 2007

I

HULLABALOO IN SPIRITUALIST CIRCLES

Winnipeg's spiritualist community is proud of the fact that it includes one of the world's foremost experts in psychic research. Over the course of just a few years, Dr Thomas Glendenning Hamilton, formerly an MP for the province of Manitoba and today chairman of the Manitoba Medical Association, has built up a formidable reputation thanks to his spiritualist work.

Dr Hamilton's interest in psychic phenomena began fourteen years ago. He was introduced to the field by one of his university colleagues, Professor Allison. His personal experience then expanded through one of Mrs Hamilton's friends, Elizabeth Poole, a remarkably talented medium of Scottish extraction. Dr Hamilton understood that the subject represented a new and infinite field of experimentation for a young scientist such as himself. He immediately began to carry out his research with unfailing sincerity and rigour, something that has always been unanimously saluted by his colleagues on all sides.

Seven years after he began organising regular séances with Miss Poole, Dr Hamilton managed to obtain his first so-called 'psychograph' or spirit photograph. This process rests on the theory that a photographic plate can be developed to reveal not only the person posing in front of the camera but also the form of a spirit, invisible to the naked eye and whose presence is only revealed once the picture has been developed. Other photographs followed and met with great success here in Canada, and also in the United States and Europe. Spiritualists consider them to be unimpeachable proof of the survival of the soul after death.

However, it should be noted that the 'teleplasm' (the term used for the substance which materialises) photographed by Dr Hamilton only represented anonymous spirits, ordinary men and women who had not known fame during their lifetimes.

Through Elizabeth Poole, contact was made with the Scottish writer Robert Louis Stevenson, the English explorer David Livingstone and the French astronaut Camille Flammarion between 1923 and 1927. But communication with these illustrious figures was limited to automatic writing where a medium writes messages for the living while in a trance, dictated by spirits. Their bodies had never been captured on a photographic plate.

However, according to Dr Hamilton himself, this time everything points to it being the spirit of Sir Arthur Conan Doyle, the great British writer, creator of the Sherlock Holmes character, who established his presence on several occasions during a series of meetings organised in spring and early summer. The face of that fervent supporter of the spiritualist cause was photographed on 27 June at a special séance, which will henceforth figure in the annals of psychic science.

Thanks to the surprising success of these experimental meetings, the status of the city of Winnipeg has suddenly been raised to that of Boston, London, New York and Paris, the traditional capitals of spiritualist research.

Dr Hamilton will resume his work in September. At this rate, the last shadows surrounding that invisible kingdom might well be removed soon and it will finally be possible to establish positively and definitively that the human soul does indeed survive after the physical death of the body.

We are grateful to Dr Hamilton for giving us an account of the séances of recent weeks, exclusively for readers of the *Toronto Daily News*. He has also entrusted us with extracts from his notes taken during the meetings where, amongst other things, the incredible dialogues between flesh-and-blood individuals and elusive spirits from the other side are transcribed. They give us a more precise idea of the materialisations and, for our most suspicious fellow citizens, allow us to judge the degree of seriousness and meticulousness the Winnipeg group has applied to its experiments.

SCRUPULOUSLY ORGANISED SÉANCES

In order to help readers picture the meetings more easily, we should specify, before going into details, that the meetings are held in a specially furnished room on the second floor of Thomas G. Hamilton's home in the centre of Winnipeg: ten wooden chairs are arranged in a circle around a solid rectangular table made of unvarnished wood, a gramophone is placed on a shelf at the back of the room and there is a wooden spirit cabinet. In two corners, opposite the psychic cabinet, a collection of photographic and stereoscopic devices with different kinds of lenses, as well as magnesium lamps used for the flashes, are permanently ready to be operated from a distance thanks to an ingenious system of remote triggers.

As Dr Hamilton has indicated, communications of this level were only possible thanks to the presence of three peerless mediums with so-called 'physical effects', that is to say the ability to produce ectoplasm, the semi-solid substance which leaves the body of the living in certain circumstances and which serves to clothe ethereal entities. In this instance they were Miss Mary Marshall, referred to in the accounts of the séance under the pseudonym Dawn; her sister-in-law Mrs Susan Marshall, referred to under the pseudonym Mercedes; and a young man who has asked to remain anonymous and who was referred to as Ewan.

As well as the mediums and Dr Hamilton, the other individuals present at the séances were W. B. Cooper, the well-known businessman; H. A. Reed, a telephone engineer for Manitoba Telephone System which contributed towards the supply and technical maintenance of the photographic and phonographic equipment; James Archibald Hamilton, Dr Hamilton's brother; Dr Bruce Chown, a paediatrician at Winnipeg Children's Hospital; Lillian Hamilton, Dr Hamilton's wife; and the businessman John D. MacDonald.

In spiritualist terminology, a spirit guide is the spirit of a deceased person who communicates with the living during a séance through the lips of an entranced medium and acts as an intermediary for contacting other spirits. To improve the quality of communication, Dr Hamilton often works with several mediums, which means that the same guide can express him- or herself through two or three different mediators in turn during a séance. In addition, for convenience it has become usual to refer to a spirit guide by attaching his name (if known) to that of the medium whose voice he is borrowing. So, in the following exchange Walter-Dawn refers to the entity known as Walter who is speaking through the medium Dawn. But Walter can suddenly decide to express himself through the medium Ewan or the medium Mercedes. He will therefore then be referred to as Walter-Ewan or Walter-Mercedes.

During the séance on 6 March (the 296th in the series of materialisations), the Hamilton group established contact for the first time with an entity claiming to be the spirit of Arthur Conan Doyle. That day, an excellent differentiated mass was recorded on a photographic plate.

The following is taken from the notes recorded during the séance:

Ewan becomes entranced.

Walter-Ewan: 'Mercedes, sit on the other side of the

cabinet beside Dawn. Don't let go of Dawn's hands.'

Mercedes, fully conscious, seats herself near the cabinet. The next half-hour is taken up with nonsense talk between Dr Chown and a Ewan trance-personality. The cameras have been ready since before the séance began.

At 9.30 Walter asks Dr Chown if he is ready to take a picture.

At 9.31 Dawn stands, bows three times, raises her right hand, holds it over her breast and speaks in a deep voice in the quiet deliberate manner characteristic of the control Black Hawk.[1]

Black Hawk-Dawn: 'Good evening, friends. Pale Face (Walter) has been with you and is still here. He is doing something for you and hopes that conditions will be satisfactory. I have just been asked to make the medium stand on her feet. She will be seated as soon as you get the message. I think from what I can see that it will not be long . . .'

(The entity ceases to dominate the medium.)

At 9.43 Dawn (entranced) very quietly says: 'One, two, three, four!'

The flash is fired on the fourth count. The exposure seems to have a very marked effect on her for she breathes very heavily. At 9.47 she again counts up to four.

Dr Chown: 'Sorry, we were ready for only one flash.'

Walter-Dawn: 'Oh, I thought you were ready for two. Place the medium on the floor, please.' (Ewan is placed on the floor.) 'Thank you. How long would it take you to get ready?'

Dr Chown: 'Sorry, I can't do another tonight. We should have received some new plates. Dr Hamilton has ordered them but I don't know when we'll get them.'

Walter-Dawn: 'Well, at least we have one picture.'

Dr Chown: 'If we get one good exposure we will be very grateful.'

The photographic plate very clearly reveals ectoplasm about eight or ten inches in length leaving the medium's mouth and flowing down towards the ground. At the top of this whitish mass, two points can be distinguished in the shape of relatively well-formed eyes with slightly dilated pupils. Darker points can be seen in each eye. The outline of white mass is well defined on the left eyebrow, while on the right eyebrow it is broken by a shadow above the outer corner of the eye. At the bottom of the ectoplasm one can make out an imperfect face with a head of hair.

SÉANCE OF 17 APRIL 1932:

A MESSAGE IN AUTOMATIC WRITING

Six weeks later, on 17 April, the following message was delivered in automatic writing through an entranced Mercedes: 'The lodger has left his box. He absolutely must return! He must! A.C.D.'

The message is obscure. Neither Walter nor any of the other spirits present that day understood its meaning. They also let it be known among the group that the entity, which claimed to be Conan Doyle, was displaying extreme agitation and seemed unable to formulate a clear and coherent message. They were nevertheless going to try to help him.

They insisted that a certain number of special séances be organised with the chosen members. A small group met on 20 April with Dawn, on 22 April with Ewan and the complete group came together on 24 April. On 27 April a hand teleplasm was recorded.

II

A MOST UNEXPECTED VISIT

M Y friend James Trelawney and I never imagined for a moment what would follow when there was a knock at the door of our rooms in Montague Street towards the end of the morning of Friday, 24 June 1932. We knew no one in London and since Miss Sigwarth, our landlady, had let someone come up without calling up from downstairs in her shrill voice – something we had asked her not to do – it probably meant that the visit was professional. It was not a moment too soon. Three months had passed with nothing to fill our days and the wait was starting to get James down.

'Mr Singleton?' a lady's voice asked my associate when he opened the door.

Hearing my name, I got up from the sofa where I had been reading and straightened my clothes, discreetly tugging my waistcoat down.

'Sadly, no, my dear lady. My name is Trelawney, James Trelawney, at your service,' my friend replied, with a slightly excessive bow. 'I am Andrew Singleton's associate. But, please, do come in. Mr Singleton will be delighted to receive you.'

When I caught sight of our visitor in the doorway, my heart began to hammer. The slender figure and the haughty carriage of the head reminded me forcibly of my late mother as she appeared in a few photographs taken more than a quarter of a century ago and for ever fixed in my mind. Fortunately, as soon as she came forward and I was able to observe her more closely, I quickly regained control of myself.

She was tall (about five foot seven) and slender, somewhere between fifty-five and sixty, and there was no doubt that she had been extremely beautiful in her youth. Under her grey woollen coat, she wore a long black dress, belted at the waist, which made her look yet more slender. Her light-brown hair was dotted with grey in places, which just underlined her natural stylishness.

She entered the main room of our flat, which served as a dining room as well as a sitting room, and looked around at its rudimentary furnishings: the table and four straight-back chairs in front of the ebony sideboard; our two desks by the window looking out onto the street, one (James's) laden with newspapers, the other (mine) overflowing with books and magazines. An old map of London hung over the stone fireplace, which separated the two parts of the room, and beyond it were the sofa, where I stood without saying anything, and two elegant armchairs on a colourful rug.

Who could be asking for me? James's name appeared first in the cards we had recently sent out. I was supposed to be his assistant.

James understood what was bothering me because he immediately came over and stood by my side. Our visitor could now study us together, which made me feel even more awkward. My friend was a kind of colossus, standing more than six foot three tall and built like a rugby player. Although we were both twenty-three, he looked older than me. I was thin and dark, whilst he was blond and muscular. Since our arrival in London, I had started growing a moustache in an attempt to make myself look older, less inexperienced.

'I am Andrew Singleton,' I said at last, stepping forward.

'If you have come to entrust us with a case, please rest assured that you have come to the right place,' James added in a professional tone.

'Thank you. But I realise that I have not introduced myself. My name is Jean Conan Doyle and—'

'Jean Conan Doyle? The widow of . . . ?' asked James, dumbstruck.

'Of Sir Arthur Conan Doyle, indeed.'

'Good heavens!' cried my friend. 'It is an honour to make the acquaintance of the widow of Sir Arthur Conan Doyle.'

James's enthusiasm seemed to amuse our guest. It should be said that my friend had a lively, cheerful personality, and people were quick to warm to him. What is more, as I had been able to judge on a number of occasions, his success with the fair sex was undeniable.

We invited Lady Conan Doyle to take a seat on the sofa, which she did with entirely aristocratic elegance, while we each took an armchair opposite her. Her striking emerald-green eyes had become sombre once more as she looked from James to me. The feverish movement of her hands betrayed a fierce agitation. She was obviously uncertain how to begin.

'I heard that you were the son of Francis Everett Singleton of Halifax,' she said suddenly, turning her gaze on me.

'You understood correctly. I am indeed Francis Singleton's son.'

'That's a relief. I have the pleasure of knowing your father. We met several times during the trips my husband and I made to America and your beautiful country, Canada.'

'I didn't know that. But, as to those meetings, and knowing your reputation, I think I would be right in suspecting that they were related to his spiritualist work?'

'You would be right,' Lady Conan Doyle replied as her face lit up again. 'And it is because of your father's spiritualist activities that I decided to appeal to his son for help, never doubting for a moment that you would demonstrate the same open-minded attitude to our ideas, which exceed the understanding of most people.'

'Well . . .' I started to say, unable to conceal my dismay. 'That's to say . . . on that particular point, Lady Conan Doyle, our views—'

'He means that on that particular point, as on all others, dear lady,' James hastened to say, 'the views of father and son are very similar, as is the nature of things. And what's more, I can assure you my views chime exactly with Singleton's.'

'Ah, if you only knew what a relief that is! It would have been impossible for me to reveal my torment to obtuse and materialistic minds.'

James leant back in his chair, aware that he had saved a situation that my sensitivity might have compromised. As always when I felt extreme vexation, I squeezed my left earlobe until it almost bled and forced myself to smile politely.

III

INTRODUCING JAMES TRELAWNEY AND YOUR NARRATOR

Y ou will no doubt have already realised that, contrary to what my friend James Trelawney had managed to suggest, I was not, at that time, an enthusiast of the spiritualist religion. For me, that 'morbid belief in the survival of the dead' was just a residual infantilism in the brains of grown-up children, grown-up children who, what is more, benefit from a very conspicuous social position, as was the case with my father.

I only discovered the details of the meetings between the Conan Doyles and my father, the wealthy merchant Francis Everett Singleton, later on. In fact, they met just twice. The first occasion was in 1914 in Halifax in the province of Nova Scotia during a trip Arthur Conan Doyle made to North America at the invitation of the Ottawa government. The second time was in 1923 during one of the numerous series of lectures on spiritualism that the writer gave around the world. On that occasion, the Conan Doyles had been invited to a dinner organised by the MP and spiritualist Thomas G. Hamilton at his home in Winnipeg. My father was on the very select guest list. He and Arthur Conan Doyle had long discussions about their respective admiration for the spiritualist movement – the writer's official conversion dated from 1916 and my father's from even further back, from 1909, although the two men were almost the same age. Lady Conan Doyle, although initially resistant to this new religion, was converted in 1919 before discovering the gift of automatic writing in 1921. At the end of the dinner, a séance was held by the medium Mary Marshall, Dr Hamilton's new protégée.

I was only three weeks old when my mother died as a result of complications in childbirth and six months old when my father was converted. I connect the two events in my mind because it is clear that for my father the death of his wife was the main reason for his spiritualist mania. What at first appeared to be a desperate attempt by a bereaved man to contact his deceased wife's spirit became a single-minded, over-riding and obsessive preoccupation, which he devoted himself to, and which was an indication of the more spiritual, even mystical, direction his life had taken. Until then, Francis Everett Singleton had been a well-known figure in high society in Halifax, Ottawa and Toronto. From what I have been told, before I was born, illustrious figures from the world of art, men of letters and politicians were often received at our house. After his conversion he saw no one, apart from a few fellow believers with whom he took part in meetings around séance tables. From that moment every minute of his existence was dedicated to communicating with spirits.

Despite our entreaties, my father always refused to let us, my three brothers, my sister and I, participate in these séances, saying that it was not a place for children, and I gradually came to doubt the veracity of those so-called communications. In the face of his persistent refusal, I responded with polite disinterest in the spiritualist cause, which over time turned into veritable contempt. Without doubt, my conduct was partly due to an automatic rejection of everything paternal; by attempting to keep any contact with his dearly departed wife for himself alone, this man, for so long admired by all, had somehow stolen what every child holds most dear. He had deprived me of the mother I had not known and whose absence would haunt my soul and wither my heart until my last breath.

However, I should clarify that, although I openly disdained my father's convictions, this did not mean I did not believe in the survival of the soul after death. On the contrary, my opinion on the subject had long been formed by reading Plato and Plutarch. It was simply that I strongly doubted that our dear lost ones had nothing better to do once they had passed over than take part in ludicrous circus tricks for a tableful of notables in their sixties.

My father was not unaware of the way I regarded him and, I am now sure, he suffered without ever letting it show. In any case, he did nothing to resolve the situation and in the end I cut myself off in silence and solitude. At the age of twelve he sent me away to boarding school at Dartmouth and I only came home at weekends. Those were the happiest days of my childhood. I learnt Latin, Greek and Italian, perfected my French and, above all, developed the taste for poetry and literature which would never leave me. I wrote my first poems at Dartmouth.

At eighteen I returned home to Halifax. But adolescence and the rebellious feelings it brings made my father's activism for the spiritualist cause unbearable to me. Wanting to escape him and the bourgeois provincialism of Halifax as quickly as I could, I decided after a few months to leave the family home and go as far away as possible, first to Ottawa and then to New York, Philadelphia, Chicago and finally Boston where I studied English literature for three years.

Boston has always been one of the intellectual capitals of the United States, with a wealth of publishers and publications of all kinds. I immediately felt at home in that immense city. What is more, it was the city of Edgar Allan Poe, the author I venerated above all others.

Outside lessons, my main occupation was reading: poetry, literature and philosophy but also history, law, mathematics and astronomy. Passionate about everything in general and nothing in particular, I was capable of devouring an ever-growing pile of books from the light-hearted to the taxing: an essay on the comparative idealism of Berkeley and Schopenhauer followed by a history of the Eskimos. I loved all genres. This immoderate taste for books clearly denoted an unfailing thirst for knowledge but it also betrayed a certain propensity to flee real life with its pain and its pleasure.

My father sought communication with souls whose territory, according to him, surrounded our physical world on all sides. I had chosen exile in the stratospheric heights of the world of ideas.

I met James Trelawney in Boston. A student like me, he was the son of a doctor originally from Edinburgh who had fled Scotland at the end of the last century. The degree in medicine he was supposed to be studying for was just a crude way of pleasing his father. For the moment James aspired to live a life of freedom, happy to find himself in a large bustling city, partial to any new adventures which presented themselves and opened up fresh prospects.

James Trelawney's real ambition was to become a detective. I had just self-published my first collection of poems and I had come to a decision: I would be a writer.

We met in a bar on Union Street where we talked for hours about detective fiction. I praised the merits of Charles Auguste Dupin and his peerless sense of analysis, which almost enabled him to solve the most difficult cases without leaving his room. James sang the praises of Sherlock Holmes with his superior scientific methods and his unique sense of observation. We did not manage to decide between them but, from that day, we were inseparable. I had found in James a sort of inverted twin, my opposite, as deeply rooted in the reality of his century as I was detached from it, a strong and positive character with incredible vitality, always ready to forge ahead but on whom I exercised a certain amount of intellectual influence. James had found in me an aesthetic and taciturn travelling companion, perhaps overly sensitive but able to analyse people and events with a certain amount of acuity, and I suspect he had the idea of using these qualities for his future work very early on.

After we had abandoned the university's lecture theatres, James suggested, as I should have expected, that I join him as a detective, arguing that with my literary talents I would be able to read between the lines of the most unsolvable criminal affairs. The idea amused me. The work left me enough time for hours of reading and writing, and it pleased me to imagine myself as a modern Dupin.

We received our few clients at rooms we rented near State Street in the centre of Boston, hoping to rival the detective agencies demanding ridiculous prices which were flourishing all over the United States in that period of economic crisis.

We were soon bored, our days almost exclusively confined to cases of adultery or pets that had disappeared. After six months, James suggested escaping an existence which had become decidedly too prosaic, and in which the criminals we dealt with demonstrated no inventiveness, and emigrating to the Old Continent. There he promised, flattering my erudition, murder was considered to be one of the *beaux-arts*. I was enthusiastic about the idea. Faithful to the memory of my hero, Edgar Allan Poe, I suggested Paris but James stuck to his guns: it would be London, the city of Sherlock Holmes.

We left New York on board the ocean liner *Mauretania* on a rainy afternoon in March 1932 and reached Southampton one freezing morning in April. We travelled to the capital by train and shortly afterwards rented the first floor of a house in Montague Street, opposite Russell Square. Miss Sigwarth, the owner, occupied the ground floor and the second floor. Apart from its location in the historic heart of London, its moderate rent and its typically British charm with its brick and stucco façade and its wrought-iron balconies, our flat had two essential qualities: it was located not much more than a stone's throw from Regent's Park – and James liked nothing better than physical exercise in the fresh air – and secondly, it was very close to the British Museum and its famous Reading Room. I could not have hoped for a better location.

Despite advertisements in the newspapers extolling our

talents, our days were no more exciting in London than they had been in Boston. The English capital under the reign of George V bore little relation to that of Victoria at the end of the previous century. That had been the London of our dreams as we read the work of Dickens, Stevenson, Oscar Wilde and Conan Doyle. Apart from anything else, fog very rarely covered the city as Londoners had long ceased heating their homes with coal, although Hollywood film directors obstinately continued to roll out the famous pea soup through their cardboard streets.

Three months after our arrival on British soil, since we were not much in demand as detectives, we began to resume our old habits: James devoted himself to his favourite sports (boxing and swimming), spending the rest of his time playing football and cricket; I spent my days with my books, at my favourite table in the Reading Room or lying on the sofa in Montague Street.

To complete these introductions, I will add that when Lady Conan Doyle visited our rooms in Montague Street she had been Sir Arthur's widow for exactly two years. In July 1930 death had separated the couple after an exclusive passion lasting more than thirty years.

Jean Leckie (her maiden name) and Arthur Conan Doyle met in 1897 when the writer was already married and the father of two children. It was love at first sight. However, faithful to the chivalrous principles of courtly love that he had made his own (courage, honesty and loyalty) and also out of guilt towards his wife who had galloping consumption and was wasting away day by day, Arthur decided that their relationship would be strictly platonic. And he kept his word, at least until 1906 when Touie died of her illness. Freed from his moral and matrimonial ties, Arthur gave himself body and soul to Jean whom he married the following year on 18 September 1907 at the church of St Margaret's in Westminster.

Jean gave him three children.

IV

A MOST UNEXPECTED VISIT (CONTINUED)

Aᶠᵗᵉʳ a moment's silence, James said encouragingly to our illustrious visitor, 'Lady Conan Doyle, we are dying to know why you wanted to meet us. If you are ready to tell us, Andrew and I are ready to listen.'

'Thank you, Mr Trelawney. What brought me here is a source of great torment to me. To tell you the truth, I can no longer sleep at night . . .'

Lady Conan Doyle briefly turned her gaze to the shelves of books on either side of the fireplace.

'I imagine you know my husband's work?' she asked.

'Oh, we have read and reread his books,' I replied, removing my hand from my ear. 'He's one of my favourite authors.'

'And I would add,' interjected my companion, 'that the character of Sherlock Holmes is what made me want to become a detective as a child. Although I now realise that the reality of the work is far less attractive than reading his stories led me to believe.'

'Oh, reality is often much more unbelievable than one might imagine, Mr Trelawney! But tell me, did you deliberately choose Montague Street?'

'Why do you ask?' I queried, surprised.

'If you are avid readers of those adventures, you will know

that this was Sherlock Holmes's first address in London. It is where he began his work as a detective before meeting Dr Watson and moving to Baker Street. My husband refers to it in one of his short stories, "The Adventure of the Musgrave Ritual".'[2]

James and I burst out laughing. I admitted it first.

'My word, Lady Conan Doyle, if ever I was aware of that, it had completely slipped my mind.'

'How hopeless we both are!' James continued. 'We will have to go back to our classics.'

'Please, gentlemen, I did not mean to offend. On the contrary, I think it is another indication of fate. It confirms that I was not mistaken in deciding to come and consult you.'

Lady Conan Doyle fell silent once again for a long moment. She was clearly trying to find the courage to speak.

Finally she resumed calmly enough, although her voice betrayed her anxiety, 'As you know perhaps, my husband died two years ago on 7 July 1930 at the age of seventy-one. The sun had just started to rise over the grounds at Windlesham when his eyes closed for ever. The night before had been very agitated. My sons and I took turns sleeping on a small sofa outside his room. Arthur did not want anyone with him. He did not want to be seen in that state.

'I should add that my husband had had his first heart attack the year before, in the spring of 1929, during a lecture tour in Northern Europe; he returned to Windlesham in a wheelchair and never really recovered.

'He was very physically diminished the week before he died but he had wanted to be part of the spiritualist delegation received by the Home Secretary with a view to repealing the Witchcraft Act.[3] The doctors tried to dissuade him but when my husband had decided to do something, no one could change his mind. The meeting was important to him. He returned home looking even weaker and older, more worn out and ill. From that day, we knew that the end was near.

'At about two or three o'clock in the morning we thought we heard murmurs and whispered cursing coming from his room but we could not identify who it was. Was it Arthur, rendered unrecognisable by his suffering? Was it the voice of someone else? My sons and I entered the room several times, intrigued by the strange mutterings, but each time we found only my husband, lying on his bed in an agitated state of semi-wakefulness. When Arthur opened his eyes, it was to try to reassure us and convince us that everything was fine and to tell us to go and get some rest.

'Later, at about four or five o'clock in the morning, just before the sun began to rise, we were alerted by groans. He was choking. We sent one of the servants to fetch the doctor. He arrived quickly and diagnosed another heart attack. Arthur could no longer say a word; the attack had left him unable to speak. Then he suddenly gestured to indicate that he wanted something to write with. Denis, our eldest son, quickly gave him a piece of paper and my husband wrote a few words on it. They were his last. After that, his soul left us once and for all.'

Lady Conan Doyle took a piece of paper folded in four from her handbag. She handed it to me. She really did appear to want me to play the leading role.

I took the piece of paper and unfolded it. In a trembling hand

Arthur Conan Doyle had written: 'The lodger is in the box and there he must stay!'

'Do you have any idea what it means?' I asked, passing the piece of paper to my friend.

'At first sight it made no sense at all,' replied Lady Conan Doyle, taking the piece of paper back from James, who had copied the message into a small notebook.

'And later?' he asked.

'Well . . . I don't know exactly how they are connected but I am convinced that what has been happening over the last few months at 221 Baker Street is not unrelated to what my husband wanted to say when he died.'

'What has been happening at 221 Baker Street?' I said, surprised. 'I thought the address didn't exist!'

'That's right, Mr Singleton. Number 221 did not exist . . . or at any rate not until twenty months ago. When my husband began to write the first adventure in the Holmes cycle the street did exist but it was shorter and stopped at Number 85. No doubt to avoid problems with a cantankerous proprietor who would not have appreciated his address figuring in a detective novel, my husband decided to house his hero at a fictitious number. However, a few weeks after Arthur's funeral, in September 1930, the City of London decided to extend the street by renaming York Place and Upper Baker Street. So one morning, Number 221 was assigned to a small brick house between Marylebone Road and Regent's Park.'[4]

'And what is the connection with the circumstances of Sir Arthur's death?' enquired James.

'For the last twenty-five years the house in question has been occupied by a retired couple, Major Henry Hipwood, who spent his entire army career in the Indies, and his wife Janet. Towards the end of last year, the Hipwoods noticed that strange events were occurring during the night in the first-floor sitting room while they were asleep in their bedroom on the second floor. The two rooms on the first floor are unoccupied; according to what I have been told, they intended to let them. They would hear footsteps and objects moving. In the morning the fact that armchairs and other furniture had been moved proved, if proof were needed, that it was not all in the owners' imagination. What is more, nothing was ever stolen or broken. The couple thought that someone must have entered their home at night and trespassed scandalously on their private property. Naturally, the Hipwoods could no longer sleep. Every night the major, who was not lacking in courage, came down from the second floor to the first as quietly as possible to confront the underhand visitor. But all it took was the sound of his slipper on the floor for all noise to stop immediately in the sitting room and Mr Hipwood was therefore never able to surprise anyone. The major's nephew, Dr John Dryden, is also a member of the SPR[5] and recounted the events in the spiritualist magazine *Light*. According to him, everything pointed to the room being under the influence of a spirit. The phenomena began four months after the new street numbering came into force and have intensified over the last few weeks. Members of the SPR suggested holding a séance in the room to try to contact the psychic being.'

Hearing this incredible tale, I began to squeeze my earlobe hard again. I had fled my country to avoid those so-called agents from the other side and here they were, tracking me down in the heart of London! Good grief! Why did all these supposedly sane and rational people feel the need to make contact with disembodied beings for every little event in their daily lives? This craze was really unbearable.

'And do *you* think it is a spirit?' I asked, clinging to a vain hope that this could not be what she thought.

'Yes, I am utterly convinced.'

I bit my lip so hard it almost bled.

'The spirit of whom? Your husband?' asked James, who seemed to relish the appearance of a ghost in the story.

'No, I am sure of that. You see, I have a certain flair for automatic writing[6] and during the many séances I have attended I have been able to contact those on the other side. Over the last two years, every day God brings I continue to try to communicate with Arthur's spirit. In vain. Something seems to be preventing him from connecting with the living at the moment. There is nothing exceptional in that; sometimes it takes several years before it is possible. But if one day he manages to contact our world, he will no doubt address his message to me, or at least someone with whom he was intellectually close during his lifetime. I cannot imagine for a moment that my husband's soul would haunt the house of a retired couple who were entirely unknown to him just because they happen to live at 221 Baker Street.'

'So, in your opinion what does it all mean?' asked James.

'I don't know. What I came to tell you is just a hunch, but a very powerful one, a strong premonition. It is possible that this intuition is inspired by the spirit of my poor husband. It is possible that this is the only means of communication he has managed to establish with me, for one reason or another. And then there are all these crimes committed in London recently. Have you read the papers this morning?'

'But a premonition of what?' I asked impatiently.

I was deathly pale and my earlobe was in danger of coming away in my hand.

'The premonition of an unprecedented tragedy, a tragedy no one is ready to confront. A tragedy where, sadly, a lot of blood will be spilt.'

Lady Conan Doyle hid her face in her hands. My friend and I looked at her, stunned. A long silence followed while we all recovered our sangfroid. When our visitor had regained control of herself, we saw that she had been crying.

'Gentlemen,' she resumed, 'since your job is to find out the truth and, what is more, your minds are not closed to what comes from the other side, I implore you to do all you can to try to understand what is happening on this side. For the sake of humanity itself!'

For the sake of humanity itself, I repeated to myself with irritation. That was really going too far.

'I must leave you,' she said, rising.

Without doubt she was still under great emotional strain because she discreetly supported herself with the back of my armchair as she passed me.

'One last thing, Lady Conan Doyle,' said James as he accompanied her to the door. 'You said earlier that while your husband was dying you heard a voice that did not seem to be his. In your opinion, could someone have entered the room without the knowledge of you or your children?'

'Somebody of flesh and blood? No, certainly not. But as for *others*, I cannot be sure.'

James and I repeated in unison: '*Others?*'

I got up in turn and joined my associate at the door. Lady Conan Doyle already had one foot on the stairs. Suddenly, as she prepared to leave my sight and my life (because, it goes without saying, I felt at that moment that it was inconceivable for James and me to get involved in such a hornet's nest), I felt the same strange sensation which had affected me when she arrived, but with even more intensity. Totally illogically, I saw my mother's face again and was extremely troubled to feel a hidden connection between the two women.

I then became vaguely aware that I might embark on the adventure.

'Here is my address and telephone number,' she said, handing me her card. 'Please do not leave me in the dark. Let me know as soon as you learn something.'

Having descended three steps, she turned and looked at me with her huge green eyes.

'Mr Singleton, a grief-stricken widow has confided her fears and anxieties to two men who were unknown to her barely an hour ago. I hope that she will not come to regret it.'

And with those moving words, Lady Conan Doyle disappeared down the stairs.

V

ANOTHER MURDER IN LONDON

'How extraordinary!' exclaimed James, once we had heard the door close downstairs.

'If someone had told me that I would travel from Boston to London to hear such nonsense I would not have believed them!' I retorted. 'And from Lady Conan Doyle no less!'

I might not have been free to decide whether to accept or refuse the case but I intended to go down fighting.

'The way I see it,' gloated James, observing through the window that our visitor was heading towards Russell Square, 'is that we finally have a case to get our teeth into. That's good enough for me!'

'What are you talking about, James? Can't you see that there is nothing credible in what Lady Conan Doyle told us? A ghost at 221 Baker Street, I ask you! Whatever next! As for the mystery surrounding the death of her husband, must I remind you that the man who died on 7 July 1930 was no longer the writer you and I so admired? He had sacrificed his career and his family for his spiritualist beliefs. He had become a phoney missionary, a cheap prophet. All he cared about was warning anyone prepared to listen of the terrible catastrophes (about which he could give no details, by the way) that were going to descend on the Western world!'

'Calm down, Andrew! Anyone would think you were ranting at your father. You have to admit that the unexplained note he wrote just before he died is extremely troubling. And what about these nocturnal goings-on at the home of the Hipwoods? If it isn't a disembodied spirit, it's up to us to find the cad who's getting his kicks from such a ridiculous game. Anyway, I've had enough of waiting for the case of the century to fall from the sky. I need action! I'm not like you; I can't lie on the sofa all day, however comfortable it may be, reading metaphysical essays and adventure stories. We've been twiddling our thumbs for three months!'

'James, I'm very much afraid that this is a hopeless case. Let's be patient. You only advertised in the papers two weeks ago. It's bound to pay off sooner or later! Look how someone came to see us today.'

'Precisely! Jean Conan Doyle came to see us!' cried my associate, pretending to be indignant. 'She came to see you! She chose to reveal her torment to you! Surely you cannot remain deaf to the appeals of a lady?'

'If we must waste our time with such futilities . . .'

I was not being very logical, it's true. I knew that this affair could not be any worse than the others that had come our way thus far. And then there was this obscure feeling involving my mother. I had to find out what it meant.

Hearing muffled footsteps on the stairs, James went to open the door and collect the pile of letters and newspapers that our landlady, Miss Sigwarth, deposited on our doorstep every morning.

'Waste our time?' he resumed, putting the post on the table

without paying any attention to it and sitting in his armchair with the day's newspapers. 'We've got time aplenty! So much so that we don't know what to do with it!'

I contemplated the plumes of blue smoke wafting from my nostrils as I ground my teeth nervously against my cigarette holder. It was one of my lucky objects, made from a very rare wood, at least according to the person who had sold it to me in a flashy boutique on Sixth Avenue in New York.

'And what's more, Lady Conan Doyle's allusion to the crimes committed here recently is melodramatic,' I said, watching a cloud of smoke dispersing. 'Scotland Yard is investigating them relentlessly and I haven't seen anything about there being a link between them. Have you read anything about it?'

James gave me a wry smile, realising that I was finally giving in. He picked up the first of the morning's papers piled on his knees and began to leaf through it.

'Here we are!' he said, pointing to an inside page in the *Daily Mail*. The headline read: ANOTHER MURDER IN THE EAST END. He skimmed the article and then whistled through his teeth.

'Well, you wanted a mystery!'

'What does it say?' I enquired, inwardly amused by my friend's heavy-handed attempt to interest me in the case.

'Read it yourself,' he replied, holding out the newspaper. 'While you do that, I'm going to see if I can find any more information in the other papers.'

The *Daily Mail* journalist described the murder of a woman during the night of 22–23 June in the small courtyard of a building in Duval Street near Commercial Street in the East End. The body of the victim, who appeared to be about forty-five and lived in furnished rooms in St George Street, less than a mile away, had been found in the early morning by one of the building's residents leaving for work. The body, lying in a pool of blood, was an appalling sight. The woman's clothes were in disarray, her skirt rucked up to her knees, and her throat had been cut so deeply that her head was only attached to her body by a small piece of skin. Chief Inspector Edward Constance of Scotland Yard had arrived on the scene half an hour after the policemen from Commercial Street police station and told the few journalists present of his disgust at such a barbaric crime, reaffirming that all necessary means would be used to arrest the lunatic.

The victim, Mary Daniels, had been an actress. She had had her moment of glory appearing at a few music halls in Shoreditch and Limehouse, and thereafter survived by her wits, including, it appeared, through prostitution. According to one of the friends with whom she had spent the evening at an inn in Spitalfields, Mary had left alone as the clock struck one, heading for her lodgings near the docks. In any case, that is what she had said. Had she intended to go somewhere else? Had she met someone en route? The old gate leading to the building in Duval Street did not lock; anyone could have pushed it open and entered the courtyard. Clearly, Mary Daniels (or the murderer) knew that and one had led the other there. The night had been mild. Had Mary thought that he was an amiable client looking for love at a price? Or had she been led there by force? At the moment, no one could say.

When I finished reading, James brandished another paper.

'An article in the *Daily Gazette* has much of the same information but its conclusions deserve our attention. Whether or not there is a proven link between all these cases, journalists are no longer afraid to establish one. Listen to this:

'Without wanting to play irresponsibly on people's feelings of fear and insecurity, the fact remains that the number of murders committed in London over the last few months, and particularly the atrocious method used, is extremely troubling. We must not forget that the death of Mary Daniels painfully echoes that of Cornelia Bancroft, aged forty, which occurred last month during the night of 12–13 May in Whitechapel near the Jewish cemetery where she was found barbarically disembowelled with her throat cut. That crime was itself reminiscent of the murder of Suzann Richardson – which passed almost unnoticed at the time – a dispossessed woman aged about fifty whose body was discovered on the outskirts of Bethnal Green on the morning of 2 April by a tram driver leaving for work. She had been stabbed seventeen times in the stomach. Finally, let us not forget that on the night of 5–6 January in a dark corner of Limehouse Causeway near St Ann's Church, the young prostitute Margaret Palmer, aged thirty, had her throat cut.'

James put down the *Daily Gazette* and, picking up the *Star*, continued: 'The journalist from the *Star* highlights the same murderous chronology but goes even further in his conjectures.

'The memory of Jack the Ripper still haunts Londoners and, citing the litany of murders committed in the capital over the last six months, it is almost as if we have been transported back forty years to the reign of the abominable killer. However, some details confirm that we have not been unwittingly subjected to lethal time travel. This time, the list of crimes perpetrated since the start of the year (not to mention last year) does not seem to be limited to the East End alone. Middle-class neighbourhoods in the West End have also experienced their share of tragedy, though to a lesser degree. Remember those two bodies found within a few days of each other in Green Park at the start of the winter, drained of all their blood. Or another case, the following week, in Jamaica Lane in Bermondsey. And another still in Chicksand Street. And remember too the prostitute atrociously mutilated in one of the bedrooms in Miss Farraday's house in Brewer Street in Soho. And the businessman found with a knife in his back, his head crushed against a table and his body viciously torn to shreds, on the top floor of a well-to-do house in Grosvenor Square. So many crimes and the investigators have no clues. And do not forget the mysterious disappearance of children over the last few weeks, reported at Hampstead police station – an abnormally high number for such a limited area, which is worrying, although care must be taken not to anticipate a tragic end for any of them at this stage. Rivers of blood are flowing along the pavements of our city and the least that can be said is that there is no end in sight.

'"Rivers of blood are flowing",' repeated James, scratching his nose. 'Lady Conan Doyle used a similar expression, I believe.'

'She said: "a tragedy where, sadly, a lot of blood will be spilt".'

'So, that is one point on which the author of this article agrees with her.'

'Or else she read the *Star* this morning before coming to see us.'

I got up and rummaged among the jumble of papers covering my desk.

'Jamaica Lane . . . Chicksand Street . . . Grosvenor Square . . .' I mused. 'It's strange, all those names remind me of something but I can't think what.'

'You probably read them in the press recently.'

'No, it goes further back. But I'm sure I've never set foot in any of those places.'

I should mention at this point that, as well as encyclopedic general knowledge, at the age of twenty-three I already had a formidable bookish memory which enabled me to remember, whenever necessary, any piece of information read in a newspaper, novel, essay or other form of print, even long afterwards.

I immediately found what I was looking for, my copy of the original edition of Bram Stoker's novel *Dracula*, published in 1897.

'Wait a minute,' I said, eagerly leafing through the book.

After a few seconds I pointed triumphantly to a passage in the book.

'Chapter XXII of the Diary of Jonathan Harker, starting on page 481: Jamaica Lane . . . Chicksand Street . . . ! These are some of the addresses where the famous Count sent his boxes containing earth from Transylvania! Hmm . . . but no reference is made to an address in Grosvenor Square. Where did I see that then . . . ?'

This time I headed for the shelf of books by the fireplace and seized a current edition of Oscar Wilde's *Picture of Dorian Gray* with a faded dust jacket.

'That's it!' I cried proudly. 'Chapter XIII describes the murder of the painter Basil Hallward by Dorian Gray, his model, who remains young and beautiful thanks to a magic pact. The body is discovered on the top floor of Gray's home, a well-to-do house in Grosvenor Square, with a dagger in his neck and his head flattened against the table.'

'You know how much I admire your literary knowledge,' said my associate with a grimace of disappointment, 'but in the circumstances I don't think it helps us much. It's probably just a coincidence.'

I had been pleased with my success. I closed the book sharply and put it back in its place.

'Oh, you're probably right. So there is nothing after all to prove that all these tragedies are connected. They are obviously crimes committed by an unbalanced person. There are more and more of them these days. We don't know why Lady Conan Doyle mentioned them. She was quite evasive about it . . .'

'In any case, a lady has asked for our help and I'm not prepared to stand by and do nothing!' announced James, with an expansive gesture. 'Especially as the lady in question is Lady Conan Doyle, for heaven's sake!'

'Very well! So, where do we start?'

'I think this calls for a visit to 221 Baker Street.'

VI

A VISIT TO 221 BAKER STREET

W<small>E</small> lunched well at our usual restaurant in Russell Square and then, as it looked as though the rain would hold off for a few hours, we decided to walk to Baker Street. Our knowledge of the real London, as opposed to the imaginary London and the districts immortalised in the literary works of the last century, was quite limited. We had bought a large copy of Reynold's Shilling Map at a second-hand shop and had hung it above the mantelpiece. The map was already slightly out of date (it was the 1899 edition and York Place and Upper Baker Street had not yet been merged into Baker Street) but it pleased us to feel that we were walking in the footsteps of the Victorians.

We went up Tottenham Court Road to Howland Street and then walked for a good twenty minutes in the direction of Baker Street. Finally, by going up Paddington Street we came to the famous street with its row of small brick houses with sash windows, standing three to five storeys high.

The area was particularly busy by Paddington Street and Crawford Street; traffic was dense and the shops, which had already reopened after lunch, were drawing in a stream of harried customers. However, there was less hustle and bustle further down the road in the direction of Regent's Park. We passed New Street on the left with its post office and, a little further on, reached No. 221. The house was three storeys high. The first floor had a narrow balcony with a railing and the corniced windows were larger than elsewhere. As so often in London homes, there was a second entrance on the lower-ground floor, hidden behind iron railings, which gave access to the kitchen and pantry.

A few minutes earlier I had been willing to bet that I would feel fairly emotional standing outside such a famous address. But strangely, once in front of the brass plaque displaying the number 221, I felt nothing. The idea that the building had inherited its great mantle by chance and that this good fortune could easily have been granted to the house next door, or any other, dampened my enthusiasm. James barely took the time to glance at the façade before hurrying to lift the doorknocker. I guessed that the place did not arouse any particular emotion in him either. And yet, with regard to the descriptions Arthur Conan Doyle had given of Sherlock Holmes's sanctuary, the Hipwoods' house was a reasonable imitation.

An imposing man aged about seventy opened the door (he was about the same height as my associate, which is saying something). He was muscular with long gnarled hands. He stared at us for a few moments, an air of authority in his grey eyes. The old soldier did not seem the type to let himself be intimidated by some noises in the night.

'Major Hipwood, I presume?' James asked.

'The very same. And to whom do I have the honour of speaking, gentlemen?' replied the retired Indies army officer.

'My name is James Trelawney and this is my colleague

Andrew Singleton. We are detectives and would like to discuss the strange events which have occurred here and are possibly still occurring on the first floor of your house. Could you spare us a few minutes?'

'I have already told the inspector from Scotland Yard who came to see me four or five months ago everything I know. I have nothing further to add.'

'Oh, but we are not from the police! We are investigating privately for Lady Conan—'

'All the more reason!' cut in Major Hipwood.

'Just a moment, Uncle!'

A slim man suddenly appeared behind the owner of the house. He looked like a weasel with his clean-shaven face and extensive baldness. I guessed that he must be about fifty. He wore round glasses, which initially gave him a comic air, but his eyes were cunning.

'You say that you have come here on behalf of whom?' asked the new arrival.

As the two colossi had temporarily dropped the ball, it was the turn of the weaker specimens to take up the challenge.

'Lady Conan Doyle,' I replied. 'She came to see us this morning and told us of the events which have occurred here. I cannot tell you more but let's just say that the mystery seems to worry her greatly and that's why she decided to call in detectives to solve it.'

'Oh, this mystery is worrying a lot of people, gentlemen! My uncle and aunt first and foremost. Allow me to introduce myself. I am Dr John Dryden. As you may have realised, I am Major Hipwood's nephew.'

'Indeed, Lady Conan Doyle mentioned you. She also said that you were an eminent member of the SPR.'

'Yes indeed! Lady Conan Doyle is a charming woman and worthy of the memory of her dear husband who did so much for spiritualism in England and across the world. Although of course more recently relations with Arthur Conan Doyle and our members were a little strained.[7] But please clarify one thing for me: I heard your name earlier when you introduced yourselves and I also note that your charming accent is remarkably similar to that of our cousins in Nova Scotia. The spiritualist movement includes an eminent member in Halifax who bears your name: Singleton. Francis Singleton.'

'Indeed, he is my father.'

'Ah!' replied the man with the weasel face, inviting us to enter the house with a wave of his hand.

Never could I have imagined that my name might open doors for me in London.

Opposite the entrance, a staircase led to the upper floors and next to it a second, straighter flight of stairs descended to the basement. The major and his nephew led us into the front sitting room where one end of a long wooden table was strewn with photographic equipment.

'I have come to take some pictures of the first-floor sitting room where the nocturnal noises and movements which have so tormented us have occurred. Would you like a glass of gin? My uncle's is excellent, I assure you.'

The major indicated that we should sit at the large table while his nephew took glasses and a bottle from an old sideboard.

'Does it happen often?' asked James, taking the glass offered to him by the doctor.

'At first,' Major Hipwood replied, 'seven or eight months ago, it only happened from time to time, always at night, in a totally irregular and unpredictable way. But now the incidents take place almost every night and sometimes during the day as well. One might say the house belongs to it!'

'Belongs to whom?' I asked.

'I have no idea. But what I do know is that *it* has almost managed to make us move out. A month ago I had to send my wife to rest at our house in Devon. She had become depressed and could no longer bear the idea of an unknown presence within our walls and, good Lord!, I can understand why! I too am starting to tire of these nights of insomnia. During my career in the Indies I fought against fearsome warriors and my courage was legendary. And yet, my nerves are starting to be affected by this elusive someone or something that no one can unmask. A week ago, it was out of the question but today, I admit, I am seriously thinking of leaving and joining my wife near Plymouth. Dear me! We didn't have all these problems when the street was still Upper Baker Street. Why the council decided to rename it I shall never know! It is this damned renumbering of the street which has caused all our problems – not to mention the letters clogging up my letterbox.'

'Letters? What letters do you mean, Major?'

In answer to my question, he stretched out his arm and opened the drawer of the sideboard, which was behind his chair. He took out an impressive pile of envelopes that he casually threw in front of us. They bore stamps from all four corners of the earth.

'All these letters are from readers of that damned Conan Doyle. Every day I receive a dozen or so letters addressed to his blasted detective: Sherlock Holmes, 221 Baker Street, London.'

'It's amazing, isn't it?' continued Dr Dryden. 'Look, there are some from Japan, Yugoslavia, Texas. I even found one the other day with a Patagonian stamp. Most of the time they want help with a mysterious crime no one can solve or the theft of a completely uninteresting trinket. And all these people are absolutely convinced that Sherlock Holmes exists!'

'What are you going to do with all these letters?' asked my associate, examining a yellow envelope from Odessa.

'Nothing for now,' said the major. Taking the envelope back from James, he pushed the pile of letters to the other end of the table. 'These phenomena on the first floor are my main concern. There will be plenty of time to resolve the other matter later.'

'Mr Singleton, I imagine that you know our Society for Psychical Research well. You know that it is a very serious organisation whose reputation extends across the world. Since it was created, it has always aimed to provide a vigorously scientific framework for spiritualist research and to see through the impostors, of whom there are sadly many these days. Since these events, which have naturally created such turmoil for my aunt and uncle, began, the most eminent members of the SPR have come to study the house with the greatest attention. And I can tell you that there is now no doubt – no doubt at all – that a disembodied spirit has taken possession of the sitting room and the bedroom on the first floor. For all of us, that is now a given.

Today, the only question remaining is who that spirit is, although I am happy to tell you that I have an inkling.'

'Really!' cried James, overplaying his admiration and desire to know. 'And would it be indiscreet to ask you what your inkling is, my dear doctor?'

'What? Arthur Conan Doyle himself of course! He appears to be the perfect suspect, if I can put it that way. Initially, 221 Baker Street did not exist. It was only his talent as a writer that made it universally known, so well known in fact that there is apparently no one on the planet unaware of the name of his hero. I think it would be the perfect place to establish contact with us from the other side.'

'More than his own home, Windlesham?' I asked.

'At the end of his life Sir Arthur exchanged some unfortunate words with the members of the SPR and I am convinced that his soul needs to repent.[8] By chance, the address of 221 Baker Street fell to my uncle and, as I am one of the best-known administrators of the organisation, it was the perfect place. What's more, given the difficulty of contacting the being which is prowling around the first floor, and if it proves to be, as I believe, the spirit of Arthur Conan Doyle, it appears that it is no easier for him to apologise to us today than it was before. Really, he was a remarkable man!'

The doctor took a sip of gin, observing out of the corner of his eye the effect his theory was having on us.

'But I still hope to contact him,' he resumed, seeing that his audience was listening attentively. 'You need to be patient with people from the other side. That is why I have come with all my equipment.'

'What? You want to take a photograph of a ghost?' asked James who, to demonstrate his incredulity, downed the rest of his gin.

'Spirit photographs, or "psychographs", are a proven technique, you know. The first pictures were obtained in the middle of the last century by an American called William H. Mumler who officiated in Boston, Massachusetts. (Would you like another glass, Mr Trelawney? Wonderful!) The practice crossed the ocean and arrived in England and then France. In Paris the plates of a certain Jean Buguet met with great success before the French authorities unjustly accused him of fraud and proceedings were brought against him in 1875. Buguet also established a studio in London, just down the road from here, at 33 Baker Street.'

'But how can a spirit be photographed?'

'A subject, preferably a medium, is placed in front of the camera because the psychic being that spiritualists call "extra" needs a lot of ectoplasmic matter in order to materialise. In theory it can be anyone as long as they are not too tense. If the being has decided to show itself, once the photograph has been taken and the plate developed, it appears next to the human subject, surrounded by a sort of fluctuating vaporous whitish halo. (And you, Mr Singleton, would you like some more gin? No, you're sure?) Usually, psychographs take two forms: either the spirit appears as he was before, without particular reference to a photograph or a portrait from his lifetime; or he "consults" a pre-existing image of himself and uses it as a materialisation model. I assure you that, in both cases, the results are surprising.'

44

'That I can well believe,' commented James, who was now wavering between uncompromising scepticism and the irrepressible temptation to believe in the impossible.

'Dr Dryden, would you mind if we watched while you take the photograph?' I asked bluntly.

'On the contrary. The medium I had requested has let me down at the last minute. Before you arrived, I was trying to persuade my uncle to participate but he did not seem very keen. You can be my subject. Even if the chances of obtaining results are poor, there's no harm trying. But are you sure you don't want a little refill first?'

Dr Dryden was decidedly partial to gin, which was rather unorthodox for a senior representative of spiritualism. As far as I know, one does not lure ghosts while smelling of gin.

'No, thank you,' I replied, indicating to James that he should decline an invitation I knew to be very attractive to him.

'Well, in that case, let's go up!'

I thought that this investigation could be brought to a close more quickly than I had imagined. If we could immediately foil the trick that the doctor and his dear uncle were cooking up, the mystery of 221 Baker Street would be solved. Really, the truth was very simple. Luck had given this house exceptional value when the street was renumbered. For the doctor and his accomplice (or accomplices – there might be more than one) creating the appearance of a ghost at an address which represented so much for readers across the world (the letters were the proof of that) was an ingenious way of earning a lot of money. It felt crooked and, surely, that rotten smell had not escaped Lady Conan Doyle.

Dr Dryden stood up and collected the camera from the other end of the table, as well as a large leather bag.

'Could one of you take that tripod over there please?'

I did so.

We followed the doctor out into the hall and climbed the stairs.

The first floor, the only one that interested us, consisted of two rooms: a sitting room which was locked and which the major opened with a bunch of keys, and a bedroom, which led off the sitting room. Light entered the sitting room from two large windows, which looked out onto Baker Street. The room contained a sideboard, a table, a sofa and an armchair. The bedroom had a single, smaller window looking over a little courtyard. Its furniture was limited to a bed, a bedside table and a large wardrobe.

Dr Dryden set his camera on the tripod near the landing door and went into the bedroom to close the blinds and create almost total darkness.

'We need darkness to develop the plates,' he explained for our benefit. 'In full sunlight the results would be worthless.'

He then took out of his bag three metal trays, what looked like clothes pegs and several glass plates, which he put on the bed.

'And what's all that?' asked James, intrigued.

'This is the developing tray and that is the fixing tray. I pour in two different solutions. The first will be used later to "develop" the latent image once the glass plate has been sensitised. The other allows me to "fix" it. It couldn't be simpler, you'll see. These glass plates are made of gelatin silver bromide. They provide remarkable quality.'

We moved into the sitting room.

'Mr Singleton, would you sit on that armchair? Like so. And you, Mr Trelawney, sit on the sofa on that side. Perfect. The light from outside is quite sufficient. Now I will adjust the focus. Wonderful. Then I insert this glass plate in the camera frame. Like so. I raise the plate frame. That's it. Now I remove the cap from the lens. Careful, nobody move! All done!'

Dr Dryden removed the glass plate from its frame and invited us to follow him into the bedroom. He closed the door and lit two candles, which he put on the bedside table.

I observed all his actions as carefully as possible. The plate he had in his hands was indeed the one he had taken out of the camera. His movements were slow and precise. The gin had apparently not had a damaging effect on his ability to concentrate. He plunged the plate into the developing tray. Nothing happened for a few minutes. Then gradually shapes began to form: a vague silhouette in a sitting position (which must be me) and another on the right (no doubt James) were gradually revealed. The shapes became increasingly sharp, the features of our faces appeared and the outline of the furniture became clearer: the table on my left, the armchair, the sofa. Finally, James and I could be seen in the photograph posed as Dr Dryden had directed. Nothing more, nothing less.

'I really do think—' I began.

'Hush – look!' Major Hipwood interrupted from behind me; I could feel his breath on the back of my head.

The vague outline of a third shape could be seen in the photograph, between James and me. Despite the precision it soon acquired, it remained vaporous and slightly translucent. It was definitely a man, tall and slender with a pointed, slightly aquiline nose, not bald but with a receding hairline. He was standing upright, behind us, slightly turned to one side, arms crossed, in indoor attire, possibly a dressing gown, and was watching the lens out of the corner of his eye, a pipe hanging from his lips.

'Good heavens!' cried James. 'It's . . .'

'It's . . . Sherlock Holmes!' I muttered.

VII

MORE CRIMES IN THE EAST END

A COLD drizzle was falling and this time we took a taxi to our
rooms in Montague Street. After the photography session
with Dr Dryden, I did not have the heart to walk.

'Well, how's that for a story! What do you think of it all,
Andrew? The ghost of Sherlock Holmes – put that in your pipe
and smoke it!'

I turned to my companion. His face was so radiant that I was
tempted not to spoil his excitement.

'What I think, James, is that we were taken in like children.'

'Taken in?' said my associate incredulously. 'You were there
with me when Dr Dryden developed the photograph. As far as
I know, he did nothing to arouse suspicion.'

'Not then, no. But there is nothing to prove that the plate he put
into his camera was not rigged. We should have checked it and we
didn't, fools that we are. The image of the actor who posed in
Sherlock Holmes's attire was probably already on the plate when
it was sensitised a second time. I have read stories about that kind
of thing in the newspapers. Most spirit photographs are rigged;
cleverly done, I admit, but tricks nonetheless. Remember the care
Dr Dryden took over placing us as he wanted us in the sitting
room, me posed in the armchair, you on the sofa. That's because
he had already planned the setting for the photograph in the

minutest detail. And he positioned us in such a way that in the frame of the lens we were perfectly placed either side of the so-called ghost. I admit that I let myself fall into the trap.'

'That's true,' admitted my friend, forcing himself to swallow his bitterness. 'Now that you mention it, all that rigmarole was very strange. But what was the point?'

'We can't be sure of anything at the moment. My opinion is that the major and his nephew want to take advantage of the potential of 221 Baker Street. The address is known throughout the world. Imagine if it were also known that Sherlock Holmes's ghost was living in the house!'

'Indeed, but the story of a ghost is still limited to the spiritualist world. No papers have reported it, I believe. And if Lady Conan Doyle hadn't told us, we would know absolutely nothing about it right now.'

'These are intelligent people who are taking their time to make sure their plan succeeds. The news will be divulged sooner or later, you can be sure of that. And the picture will help give it credibility in the eyes of the public.'

'Hmm . . . and where is Lady Conan Doyle in all this? Do you think she is in cahoots with them?'

'I tend to think not. But we cannot exclude the idea.'

James clenched his jaw. He profoundly regretted letting himself be blinded by the sensational nature of what we had witnessed. My friend was open and impulsive. I would not have wanted to be Dr Dryden if their paths had crossed just then.

'Oh, Andrew, of course you're right! Those spiritualists are truly incorrigible scoundrels!'

The taxi dropped us in front of our lodgings. Having paid,

we were preparing to open the door to Miss Sigwarth's house when we heard the newspaper boy shouting his refrain: 'Special edition! More murders in the East End! Two women found brutally murdered!' I signalled to the boy who was standing a dozen yards down the road on the southern corner of Russell Square.

'It was a busy night,' I said, waving the unfolded newspaper in front of James. 'The forces of evil have struck again apparently.'

MORE MURDERS IN THE EAST END, screamed the headline on the front page of the evening edition of the *Daily Gazette*.

When the door to our rooms was closed, I threw myself on the sofa and began to read the article in question aloud.

'Last night the East End was again subjected to its lot of death and horror. Two murders were committed, close to one another and at an interval of only a few hours.

'First was Anna Leigh, a 47-year-old prostitute, who was found at daybreak in Ellen Street in Whitechapel by a fruit and vegetable seller heading for Petticoat Lane market where he worked from his cart. The victim's body was lying on the pavement in a doorway and her throat had been slit. Her skirts had been raised to reveal the stomach and the genital area, which had been dreadfully mutilated. Anna Leigh lived a few streets away in furnished rooms in Turner Street near the London Hospital. Miss Harvey, the manageress of the building, described her as a decent and intelligent woman who had been reduced to her current state of poverty by a tragedy which occurred a few years ago. Two witnesses confirmed that they had seen the prostitute that night. The first, who knew her well, saw her with a seaman on Commercial Road at about midnight. The second, a policeman on his beat, confirmed that he had come across the victim alone in Anthony Street at about one o'clock in the morning. The modus operandi was reminiscent of the murder of Mary Daniels the night before and, to a greater extent, the murder of Cornelia Bancroft during the night of 12–13 May, although officially the police are still not attributing all the murders of the last few weeks to the same individual.

'But will the Metropolitan Police Superintendent's calming words be enough to prevent panic spreading this time? It is doubtful because, in the early hours of this decidedly bloody 24 June, at the very moment when Scotland Yard inspectors were investigating the murder of poor Anna Leigh in Ellen Street, a rag-and-bone man had just discovered another body in Mitre Square and was hurrying to one of the police stations in the City to raise the alarm. The officer in charge was woken and, in view of the gravity of the situation, went to see for himself the site of the tragedy. The body of a blonde woman, aged about thirty-five and whose identity remains unknown for now, was lying in front of the railings of the old abandoned warehouse on the corner of Mitre Square. Her face had been torn to shreds and her abdomen had been ripped open from her chest to her stomach. However, unlike the murder of Cornelia Bancroft whose entrails were placed by the body in a despicable pyramid of flesh, this time the murderer had not removed the internal organs. There were indications that he had been disturbed in his work. To help them in their enquiries, the police are counting on a statement made by a witness who came forward of his own accord at Bishopsgate police station. He stated that at 3 a.m. precisely he had seen a man wearing a long black coat in the company of a blonde woman near Mitre Square. The woman was clearly crying and trying to get away from her companion. The witness says that he approached them to try to intervene but the stranger struck him violently with his hand, knocking him to the ground and rendering him unconscious for a few seconds. However, before being struck he apparently observed to his great amazement that the black coat was covering not a man of flesh and blood but "a kind of shapeless, bloodless, vaporous monster". The implausibility of his description is no doubt due to the hard knock to the head he received; the man was clearly no longer in possession of all his faculties. Nonetheless, let us hope that this courageous citizen's memory returns quickly because, so far, this is the only credible witness statement the police have to help them solve a series of crimes which, alas, do not yet seem to be at an end.'

The sombre details of these murders immediately reminded me of things I had read before and I turned to my associate in excitement.

'The *Star* journalist this morning didn't know how right he was when he made the connection between these murders and Jack the

Ripper's crimes. These latest two murders are exact replicas of those of Elizabeth Stride and Catherine Eddowes, committed on 30 September 1888. I remember perfectly reading a detailed description of them in the Public Library in Boston in the memoirs of one of the policemen in charge of the investigation.'[9]

As I lit a Russian cigarette and inhaled its acrid smoke, trying to imagine what this 'shapeless, bloodless, vaporous' murderer could be, there were three sharp knocks on the door to our rooms. James, who was thoughtfully pacing up and down in front of the sofa, opened the door to our landlady.

'This letter just came for you,' said the shrill little voice.

'Thank you very much, Miss Sigwarth. I wish you an excellent evening!' James replied with ceremony before closing the door and nimbly tearing open the envelope on which was written in capital letters: FOR MESSRS SINGLETON AND TRELAWNEY, 46 MONTAGUE STREET.

The following message was written in purple ink on a large sheet of white Bristol paper bearing the emblem of the Society for Psychical Research:

Holland Park, 24 June, 6.10 p.m.

Dear Sirs,

I have just reported back to my colleagues at the SPR as to the results of the incredible photography session this afternoon at 221 Baker Street, which providence desired you to witness.

It has been decided that a spiritualist séance should be organised on the first floor of that house as soon as possible to confirm the presence of the psychic being whose image we captured and that an attempt should be made to contact him.

As well as my uncle and myself, three individuals affiliated to our society will be present, together with a medium of proven abilities who is recognised in the best London circles. I very much hope you can join us. The spirit has decided to show himself now after eight months of complete silence and your presence may have played a role in that decision. Whatever the case may be, we must give ourselves the best chance.

I will expect you this evening at 11.30 p.m. at Major Hipwood's house. Please be punctual. We are possibly on the verge of a great breakthrough.

Yours faithfully,

Dr John Dryden

'He doesn't waste any time, does he, the scoundrel!' cried James, looking up from the letter.

'This is perfect. We were wondering what to do to unmask Dr Dryden and here he is giving us the opportunity himself! There will be six of them and only two of us. We must be vigilant, my dear friend, keep our eyes open and observe all their movements. This time we will not be taken in.'

'I love it when you talk like that!' said James, stretching his long arms. 'Nothing like a ghost hunt for a little light exercise. Eleven thirty? That leaves us plenty of time to catch our breath . . .'

Admittedly, we had not had such a busy day for a long time. In truth, I was even starting to get a taste for all this new activity. The intellectual stimulation and the thrill of the unknown were actually rather agreeable. What's more, I was well on the way to confounding one of those spiritualists whose woolly theories had been poisoning the century.

I grabbed a few books off the shelves, which I thought would help our case, particularly the complete edition of the Holmes series published by John Murray in 1928, and then made myself comfortable on the sofa in the sitting room.

VIII

A SURPRISING SPIRITUALIST SÉANCE

WE were expected at 221 Baker Street in a little under ten minutes. Our taxi was speeding down Oxford Street. The sky had been threatening rain all evening but it had been considerate enough to wait until we had left and now it sounded like a drum roll as drops fell in squalls onto the canvas roof of the Austin 7.

At the junction between Oxford Street and Charing Cross Road, the cab stopped at a red light. James and I became intrigued by a group of about a dozen people who were making a commotion, cursing and swearing, on the other side of the road as they sheltered under their umbrellas. Since we had left Montague Street the pavements had been deserted. In such inclement weather only something major could have caused such a furore in public.

James asked the driver to turn around and stop the car in front of the crowd.

'I say, gentlemen!' he called, lowering the window and looking annoyed as the cold rain splashed his face. 'Has something happened?'

'Indeed!' replied a man dressed in a black suit and a bowler hat. 'An MP, Thomas Blunden, has just been murdered. I was nearby when the body was found. It happened barely half an hour ago in an alleyway off the Strand near the Thames. Now the area is completely cordoned off. Apparently, the murderer beat his victim with a cane until he died. Poor Blunden, he was seventy-three! How could he defend himself against such a brute?'

'Has the attacker been found?' I asked.

'No,' said another man, older and also angrier. 'He could be sitting calmly in a tavern in Aldwych right now, sipping a glass of hot gin, while our policemen come up with their theories. This man must be caught and caught quickly. The murders keep coming, night after night, and no one is ever arrested. It's incomprehensible. Our women and children are in danger. Something must be done!'

'Thank you for the information,' cut in my friend, indicating to the driver to move off.

'He's right that the number of murders is increasing,' James commented when we were once more on the move.

'And the police aren't exactly covering themselves in glory,' I said, looking at my watch. 'Now we're late.'

'We're nearly at Baker Street. We'll be there in a minute. Oh! If you only knew how exciting I find all this! Have you already taken part in a séance?'

'No. When I was a child and I begged my father to let me participate in one of his meetings, he refused. Later on, it was me who was firmly opposed, to his great disappointment. But he repeatedly told me how things were organised and then I read a lot of articles written by anti-spiritualists who took a malicious pleasure in revealing the tricks and subterfuges used during these séances. So remember, we must pay close attention to each guest, observe all their movements. Nothing must escape us. Nothing!'

We had just arrived outside the Hipwoods' red brick house. A light could be seen on the ground floor in the front sitting room where the major and his nephew had received us earlier. We could also make out a faint glow in the sitting room on the first floor where we had posed in front of the camera.

'Don't worry,' resumed James, paying for the journey. 'We may have been tricked this afternoon but I don't intend to let it happen a second time. Wring their necks more like!'

At the first knock, Dr Dryden himself opened the door.

'Good evening, gentlemen. You are very punctual, the clock in the sitting room has just sounded the half hour. Please do come in.'

The doctor showed us into the sitting room where five people (four men and a woman) were seated, each with a glass in hand. Among them was Major Hipwood at the end of the table. He towered over his neighbours by more than a head. At our entrance, everyone stood up.

On the major's right was a young man with short, lightly slicked-back brown hair, dressed in his Sunday best. His attractive, gentle face betrayed a profound melancholy and revealed the temperament of a poet, deeply emotional, more used to spiritual exercises than worldly recreations. He was also the only person drinking orangeade.

Next to him was an elderly lady, austere and with carefully arranged white hair, who often turned her gaze on the young man with the gaunt face. She seemed very concerned about his well-being.

Next to the lady was a tall clergyman – the only one apart from James who was not put to shame by the major's height. He was very thin, aged about sixty and dressed in a severe flannel suit.

Finally, next to the clergyman, a man of about forty with curly hair and a skilfully combed moustache was fidgeting in his seat and wringing his hands. It was clear from watching him fidget that he was not naturally composed. Although shorter than average, he was remarkably well-built and the muscles in his arms and shoulders bulged under the fabric of his shirt.

'Mrs Lang, gentlemen,' said Dr Dryden, turning to the other guests, 'let me introduce Andrew Singleton and James Trelawney, the two detectives who were present at the photography session this afternoon. As I told you, they are investigating the psychic phenomena at 221 Baker Street at the request of Lady Conan Doyle, whom I believe you all know.'

At the name of our visitor, a slight smile appeared on the faces of the clergyman and the weightlifter.

'Mr Singleton, Mr Trelawney, let me introduce those with whom we will carry out the séance this evening. You already know my dear uncle, Major Hipwood, the owner of the house, who has agreed to join our group. Sitting next to him, our medium for this evening, Horace Lang, and his charming mother, Mrs Elena Lang, who always accompanies her son to the séances he participates in to make sure he comes to no harm. And so much the better because Mr Lang, despite being so young, is one of the most brilliant mediums I have ever met. He is also – it goes without saying, as you cannot have one without the other – one of those who gives the most of their person. Next to Mrs Lang is the Reverend Jerome Stanford who, as well as ministering to his parish, devotes his free time to psychic research. He is one of its leading ambassadors. And, finally, next to him is Clive Randall, one of the largest tobacco traders in England who has also devoted a lot of energy (and goodness only knows, he has a lot of it!) to the success of our mission, informing men of what to expect after their death and how to go about rebirth on the other side. But I am talking too much! These gentlemen must be thirsty! You will have a glass of gin of course?'

'No, thank you,' I replied. 'It is already late and I admit that I am eager to see Mr Lang at work.'

'So am I,' added Clive Randall, seeing that Dr Dryden was about to fill his empty glass. 'What's more, I imagine that Reverend Stanford, as is his habit, is going to report on the details of our séance in one of his precise and scrupulously written articles. It is perhaps not desirable to read in the next issue of *Light* that this meeting was saturated with alcohol as the work began.'

All the other guests laughed at the joke, apart from Dr Dryden, who raised his eyebrows and put the jug of gin down sharply on the table.

'Well, if everyone is agreed,' he said, 'we can begin.'

'Dr Dryden told us that you were Francis Singleton's son,' Reverend Stanford said, turning to me. 'I imagine that you are *au fait* with how these meetings are organised.'

'Let's just say that I have attended several séances organised by my father at our house in Halifax,' I lied, hoping to suggest from the outset that I was not someone to be trifled with. 'But I do not claim to be a specialist, far from it.'

'And you?' Mr Randall asked James.

'Oh, I'm a complete novice. But a curious novice who just wants to watch and, above all, learn!'

'You have chosen a good moment,' continued the clergyman. 'You know, we spiritualists are always rather hesitant about welcoming strangers to a séance. You never know, if you will excuse the expression, *who you will end up with*. The magnetic flow, which circulates around the room where the medium works, is extremely sensitive to influences of all kinds. If we include someone who does not believe in spirits and who is obstinately seeking additional reasons not to believe, the chances of success are considerably reduced. But since you are the son of our eminent colleague, I presume that there is nothing to fear in that respect.'

For a moment I wondered whether the reverend had seen through us and understood our real motivation but he gave me a broad smile and cordially led me over to the rest of the group, which had already moved towards the first floor. My concerns appeared to be unfounded.

Upstairs, the layout of the sitting room had been changed to host the spiritualist séance. The table and armchair had been removed – maybe they were in the adjoining bedroom. The sofa had been moved to the other side of the room between the two windows and over it a heavy brown curtain had been rigged up with a system of curtain rails, giving it the air of a Red Indian tepee. In the middle of the room eight wooden chairs had been placed in a circle, relatively close to one another, apart from those on either side of the sofa – as if someone were waiting behind the curtain and a path had been left for him to come forward to the middle of the circle.

'Mr Lang,' began Dr Dryden, 'I suggest you sit to the left of the psychic cabinet as usual. Mrs Lang, please sit next to your son. Clive, next to Mrs Lang, then Mr Trelawney, Uncle, Reverend Stanford and Mr Singleton. I will complete the circle on the other side of the cabinet.'

We obeyed these instructions and sat in our appointed places.

'What does that do?' asked James, pointing to the tent.

'That is what we call a "spirit cabinet" or "psychic cabinet",' replied the doctor. 'It enables the ectoplasmic vapour which escapes from the entranced medium's body to be condensed and stops it being wasted. Spirits find it difficult to physically show themselves to us. They need that thick, semi-luminous vapour, which can be solidified at will and take all possible forms. It is a valuable commodity that should not be inconsiderately wasted. Our friend Mr Lang is an excellent producer of ectoplasm. That is why he has such a good reputation.'

The young Horace Lang blushed at Dr Dryden's compliment and prepared to add something but his mother was quicker.

'The production of ectoplasm is very gruelling. My son is constantly asked to assist in the materialisation of spirits and I would like to repeat that it is imperative to reduce the number of séances he participates in – for the good of his health. Horace is not yet twenty, let me remind you!'

'We do understand,' responded Reverend Stanford. 'The health of your son is more important than any other consideration. And all of us at the SPR are extremely impressed by your determined commitment to ensure your son enjoys continued good health. We will, I assure you, agree to a pace which suits you.'

'Generally speaking, Mrs Lang,' Dr Dryden went on, 'the calendar of séances is planned with care. Our haste to carry out this one was due purely to the exceptional nature of what happened here this afternoon.

'Well,' he resumed after a moment's silence, 'Reverend Stanford and Mr Randall checked the spirit cabinet earlier. They have judged it to be perfectly in keeping—'

'One moment please,' cut in James. 'I imagine, Doctor, that you won't mind if we check ourselves that everything is indeed in order?'

'You are quite right, Mr Trelawney. Gentlemen, if you wish to do so . . . ?'

James and I got up from our seats and lifted the curtain covering the spirit cabinet. Inside, the space was very small. A short man would find it difficult to stand upright. As for hiding in the folds of the curtain or behind the sofa, it was unthinkable.

I whispered surreptitiously in James's ear, 'Everything will happen in darkness. Don't let go of Clive Randall's hand for a moment, or the major's. I will do the same with the reverend and the doctor.'

James winked in agreement.

'Are the landing door and the one to the bedroom still accessible?' I asked, turning back to the group.

'No, of course not. The bedroom has been locked. And the major can now lock the landing door. Uncle?'

The major immediately obeyed his nephew's request

and, taking a bunch of keys from his jacket pocket, locked the door.

Reverend Stanford and I went to check the bedroom door while James and Mr Randall ensured that access to the landing was impossible.

'Everything seems fine,' I said, returning to my seat.

'Since everything appears satisfactory, we can begin. May I remind our guests that we must avoid crossing our legs so as not to risk interrupting the fluids. Sit up straight in your chairs. Mr Randall, would you mind switching off the light? Perfect. I suggest we now hold hands.'

'Do we have to sit in darkness?' asked James.

'The ectoplasmic vapour is very sensitive to light. Darkness is far preferable. In general, we work in total darkness. Here, we can see a little because of the light from the street. But I know from experience that a little light reassures novices.'

After a few minutes, during which I could see nothing around me, the outline of the guests began to take shape. Opposite me, a little to the left, I could quite clearly make out the silhouettes of the major and my friend, as well as the easily identifiable white hair of Mrs Lang between her son Horace and Mr Randall. By turning my head ninety degrees to my right, I could see Dr Dryden beside me, his slightly moist hand in mine, and on my left the hieratic Reverend Stanford.

After a few minutes, we heard someone gasping for breath and I noticed the medium's frail figure literally convulse on his chair.

Gradually a strange feeling crept over me. It was my first time in a spiritualist circle and I suddenly found myself being reminded of all those séances in which my father had participated in order to contact his dearly departed wife. What if he had succeeded? What if he had been telling the truth?

'Horace is going into a trance,' commented the doctor. 'You can speak if you have something to say. There is nothing worse than a silence full of misunderstanding.'

'Is he suffering?' asked James.

'Suffering? No,' replied Mrs Lang. 'But it tires him out. His spirit leaves his body if you like. Then a spirit can use it as it wishes to communicate with us. Sometimes Horace loses six pounds in a single meeting!'

'Listen! I can hear a voice!' exclaimed Clive Randall. 'I think it's Blanche!'

A feeble murmur could indeed be heard but I could not say where it was coming from.

'Blanche is one of the spirits with whom we tend to be in contact,' explained the doctor. 'She acts as a guide in our communications with the other side. Without the aid of these controllers, all our efforts would be in vain. Blanche? Are you there, Blanche?'

'Yes, I am here,' replied a gentle voice, which did not sound like any of the people present, even in disguise. 'I see that you have guests. Welcome!'

Her breath appeared to move about the room, first in the centre of the circle and then slowly passing around us. But each guest was in his place and I could see no shadows or suspicious movements.

'Blanche, let me introduce Mr Andrew Singleton and Mr James Trelawney. They are our friends and, like us, are trying to solve a certain mystery.'

'Good evening, Mr Trelawney. Good evening, Mr Singleton. Oh, Mr Singleton! I can feel amazing warmth within you. Are you feeling well?'

'Go ahead, Singleton. Answer her. Please do not be afraid to speak.'

As I heard the voice talking to me, my hair immediately stood on end. However much I had tried to convince myself that the artifice was childishly simple, that all it needed was someone hidden in a corner of the room that I hadn't seen – unless it was just a recorded voice or something of the kind – I was overwhelmed by emotion.

'I feel great distress in Mr Singleton. Death worries him, I believe. Rest assured, Mr Singleton, the person of whom you constantly think is near me. She cannot talk to you, it is not yet the time, but please know that she is happy. She asks me to greet you. And to tell you that she loves you dearly!'

I almost crushed the reverend's hand and the doctor's. No doubt used to this kind of nervous reaction, they firmly resisted the pressure.

'Calm down, Mr Singleton,' the doctor told me. 'You will make her leave. Do you want to ask Blanche any questions? Make the most of this moment!'

Yes! Of course I wanted to talk to her! But the words would not come. I was incapable of speech.

'Blanche,' Dr Dryden resumed, filling the silence, 'we are here because strange events have been occurring in the house of my uncle, Major Hipwood. We are convinced that a spirit has taken possession of this room. Can you help us?'

'Indeed,' said the voice, passing close by my chair. 'The

room you are in is inhabited by a powerful spirit. Actually, he is next to me as we speak. He is listening to you.'

'Is it the spirit who appeared in the photograph the doctor took this afternoon?' asked Clive Randall.

'Yes.'

'Is it possible to contact him now?'

'Yes. He wishes you to know that he intends to materialise. It will only take a few seconds.'

At that moment, something more startling than anything I could have imagined took place in front of my eyes. The curtain of the psychic cabinet started to move as if there were a draught and then the two sides of the material slowly opened, revealing between the motionless bodies of the medium and Dr Dryden a cloud of whitish vapour which came towards us and grew thicker. One thing I could be sure of, thanks to the feeble light from outside, was that none of the guests had risen from their seats.

'The spirit is materialising,' murmured the doctor. 'Look, he is still growing.'

The luminous column was indeed continuing to expand. It slid right into the middle of the circle, vacillating and pulsating like a beating heart. Then, gradually, it took on the shape of a man of about forty, around six feet tall, erect, lean and wiry, with a fine mouth and grey penetrating eyes. The surprisingly malleable matter continued to solidify until it revealed with striking precision the small checks of a tweed suit apparently made of gauze. It was undoubtedly the same spirit as the one in the photograph.

'Can you speak?' asked the doctor.

'Of course,' replied the spirit in a loud, deep voice. 'Usually, I am the one who asks the questions. But this time I am resigned to making an exception. I understand that it will make life easier. It's only that this room is so peaceful when you are not here!'

'Exactly!' erupted the major. 'This room belongs to me and I do not wish to see someone trespassing, however disembodied he may be.'

'Ha-ha! Don't take it like that, my dear man. Even when I was alive I preferred renting. And I was always on excellent terms with my previous landlords. There is no reason why it should be different with you.'

'Come, Uncle,' cut in Dr Dryden. 'Our friend is a gentleman, let us behave like gentlemen. But you have not told us your name. Would it be indiscreet to ask you?'

'My name is Holmes. Sherlock Holmes, ladies and gentlemen.'

He bowed several times. I could see the other guests through his transparent ectoplasmic body.

'But Sherlock Holmes never existed!' pointed out Clive Randall. 'It is well known that the character was invented by Arthur Conan Doyle. I do not see how we could have the spirit of an imaginary detective before us!'

'Really? And yet, I assure you that is the case.'

'Are we to understand,' asked James, 'that Sherlock Holmes really existed? That he was not invented by the author? Better still, that you served as a model for Conan Doyle?'

'Hold on!' The spirit roared with laughter. 'I said I was prepared to answer a few questions, not be subjected to an interrogation. Remember that I am mainly here to negotiate the rent with my friend the major.'

'Do you meet Arthur Conan Doyle in your world?' James continued.

'No. Sir Arthur and I are not on very good terms.'

'Why?'

'That is not your concern.'

I was completely powerless as I witnessed this scene. I had focused all my logical faculties on trying to understand how the subterfuge worked but I could not explain how it was technically possible to make such a false human being appear, move, react and even tell jokes. The grey and white shades of the apparition almost brought to mind yet another cinema adaptation of the adventures of the famous human bloodhound. Except that it was not a film character in front of my eyes and nowhere could I see the hidden projector. It was neither Arthur Wontner, nor Eille Norwood, nor John Barrymore, whose acting I admired. It was real and to my astonishment I was witnessing an actual spiritualist séance, my brain paralysed by a ceaseless deluge of questions. What if my father was right? What if the spirits of the dead were indeed among us? What if . . . ?

Luckily, James had kept his sangfroid.

'Mr Holmes, since you claim to be the spirit of the great detective, you cannot be insensible to the bloody tragedies which are disturbing London at the moment.'

'What do you mean?'

'I am talking about this terrible series of murders. The police seem overwhelmed and—'

'Scotland Yard has always been overwhelmed!'

'. . . and it really needs an enlightened spirit like yours.'

The spirit's milky face showed some confusion.

'How many murders have been committed?'

'Difficult to say. Several dozen, probably; in any case no fewer than four in the last two days. And coming here in a taxi, not even an hour ago, we learnt of the death of a Member of Parliament. The tragedy had just occurred in a deserted alleyway off the Strand.'

'Hit with a cane?'

'Until he died.'

'Hmm . . . and the other crimes?'

'Some seem to be re-enactments of those committed by Jack the Ripper more than forty years ago. The victims are mostly prostitutes, often disembowelled, always dreadfully mutilated, and always within a one-mile radius of Whitechapel, the sinister epicentre. But there have also been mysterious disappearances of children in Hampstead, bodies found drained of their blood near Green Park, Jamaica Lane—'

'And Chicksand Street?' finished the spirit.

'Exactly! Chicksand Street. So you do know something about it then?'

The apparition appeared deep in intense deliberation. He began to pace up and down jerkily and tensely in the middle of our little group, ceaselessly rubbing his forehead. Under other circumstances, I would have laughed to see that such agitation was not just the privilege of the living.

'No, no and no!' he suddenly broke out, turning to James and looking at him with an icy expression. 'I can do nothing for you. The police must handle it alone – I'm sorry!'

He turned on his heel, deciding to cut the séance short.

'Mr Holmes!' called Dr Dryden, who was visibly angry at how the interview had gone. 'Stay with us, please.'

'I have nothing further to add. Leave my sitting room, all of you! I never want to see you again! And there is no point trying to contact me again!'

The figure had barely disappeared behind the material of the spirit cabinet when we saw his light hair poke through the curtains again. This so-called Holmes quickly glanced at our group and then focused on my associate.

'The only advice I can give you, my young friend, is to go to Narrow Street near Limehouse Causeway tomorrow night between midnight and one o'clock. You may be able to prevent another name being added to the list of victims. And now, ladies and gentlemen, I bid you good night!'

His head vanished.

'Clive, turn on the lights!' ordered Dr Dryden.

The bright light of the ceiling lamp flooded the room, forcing me to close my eyes for a few seconds.

James immediately leapt out of his seat and lifted the curtain of the psychic cabinet but, of course, he found no one inside.

On his chair the medium came back to life slowly under the attentive care of his mother.

I felt groggy. I had just experienced the most trying minutes of my entire life. I returned to Montague Street in complete silence.

IX

JAMES REVIEWS THE CASE

THE following day, Saturday 25 June 1932, it was nearly midday when I got up, feeling tired, my mind fuddled. When I entered the sitting room James was in the middle of doing his daily exercises in a vest and long johns.

My friend's vitality did not surprise me. If his expression was anything to go by, the surprising *coup de théâtre* the day before had obviously not disturbed his sleep. On the contrary, I guessed that he was delighted with the direction our case was taking. A ghost story and the ghost was none other than Sherlock Holmes. Any human bloodhound worthy of the name would pray for such an enigma to present itself.

The remains of breakfast were still on the small low table in front of the sofa. I sat down and had a few slices of toast and muffins prepared by Miss Sigwarth which, amazingly, James had left for me, despite his voracious appetite.

It goes without saying that I had had little sleep. Put yourself in my place. In less than twenty-four hours, from Lady Conan Doyle's unexpected visit to the spiritualist meeting, it might be said that events had been conspiring to tear my well-established certainties to shreds. Overnight, I had had to reconsider my position on a series of issues (life after death, the existence and manifestation of spirits, communication with the other side, etc.) and sign up to doctrines that I had always fundamentally denied, at least in that form. But this time it was difficult not to agree with them. Truly, I had played and replayed the events of the nocturnal séance at 221 Baker Street a thousand times in my head but I invariably came to a conclusion which, the day before, had seemed complete nonsense: it was indeed a disembodied spirit which had appeared before us. It was impossible for Dr Dryden to have manipulated James and me to that extent and tricked us with an entirely fake apparition. And had I been tempted to deny the evidence, Blanche's voice was there to remind me of the most important element. Through that spirit guide, Leonor Singleton had contacted me, she had spoken to me, she had given me a message! Imagine – the first words from my mother since I had been born! Without wanting to admit it, it felt as if I had been waiting all my life for a moment like that. And maybe that violent refusal to believe in invisible things, the head-on opposition to my father's theories had been dictated by excessive pride, blind arrogance. The truth had always been within me, hidden, silent, but oh so present! It had just been waiting for the right moment to break out.

'Come on, Andrew! You should be pleased that death is not the end of everything and that another life awaits us. In any case, as you can see I have decided to redouble my efforts. If you have to die one day, you may as well die in good shape!'

James finally stopped moving about and, with a towel around his neck, threw himself into the armchair opposite me.

'I got up early this morning to take stock of our case. Do you want to hear my thoughts?'

'Please go ahead.'

He adopted a learned and serious air whose incongruence with his sporting get-up would have made me roar with laughter under other circumstances.

'Well, let's start at the beginning. On the one hand, we have the death of Arthur Conan Doyle from a heart attack according to the doctor, but the writer's wife claims that the death is part of the mystery. Another voice, not her husband's, was heard on several occasions in the dying man's bedroom that night. When she or one of her sons tried to find out where the voice was coming from, they drew a blank. In support of Lady Conan Doyle's intuition, we only have this strange note written by her husband before he died: "The lodger is in the box and there he must stay!"'

'As far as intuition goes, I think we can trust Lady Conan Doyle.'

'Well, well! I'm glad to see that yesterday's séance managed to overcome your down-to-earth positivism.'

'Let's just say that I did her an injustice.'

'Good of you to admit it. During her visit, Lady Conan Doyle also claimed that the death of her husband was connected, in a way she did not specify, to the mystery at 221 Baker Street. We must therefore ask ourselves how that could be. In other words, what is the connection between the death of Arthur Conan Doyle and the ghost of Sherlock Holmes who appeared at the séance? You agree, Andrew, that we can reasonably think that it was indeed a phantom?'

'We can at least suppose it. On the other hand, there is nothing to prove that the ghost is that of Sherlock Holmes.'

'But you saw him as well!' retorted James. 'The physical

details of the spirit corresponded perfectly to Conan Doyle's descriptions of his character: thin, an aquiline nose, a prominent square chin . . .'

'Hmm. Several million disembodied souls in the vast territory of the other side might fit that description. How do we know that it wasn't an anonymous and idle spirit trying to trick us?'

'My word, Andrew, you're determined to think the worst, aren't you! Yesterday, we were supposedly John Dryden's dupes. Today you're talking about a mischievous spirit who enjoys playing tricks on us!'

'You're right,' I replied, a little annoyed. 'I'm already falling back into my old habits. But if we admit that this spirit spoke the truth, then we have to conclude that Sherlock Holmes really existed. I cannot believe that is true, you know.'

'Until yesterday we would have supposed that 221 Baker Street didn't exist either!'

'That's not the same thing.'

'Imagine,' James continued, 'that Arthur Conan Doyle was a kind of chronicler and that in his work he just reported the cases investigated by a Sherlock Holmes who was actually alive!'

'If the man was as talented as his adventures lead us to believe, he should have been known throughout the world – as his literary alter ego is.'

'Maybe Sherlock Holmes wasn't his real name. Maybe he preferred to stay in the shadows to continue working incognito.'

'But the ghost introduced himself with that name.'

'The chap has the theatrical instinct. If he had introduced

himself using his real identity, we would not have known who he was! You have to admit, the spectacle would have lost some of its thrill!'

'Fine. So the question is, who is hiding behind the pseudonym of Sherlock Holmes? Or rather who was hiding? Because, if we really saw a ghost, the fellow has passed over.'

'That's what we have to find out. And was this phantom the person Lady Conan Doyle thought she heard talking to her husband the evening before he died? Remember that when I asked her if someone could have entered the room she replied: not someone "of flesh and blood".'

'I remember perfectly.'

'Conan Doyle is considered to be the creator of the Sherlock Holmes character. If it turns out that he just reported someone else's cases, a simple Dr Watson if you will, that changes everything! Maybe, for reasons we don't know, the ghost of the real Sherlock Holmes threatened that night to reveal everything to the general public. Upset by the idea that his subterfuge might be revealed, the poor writer's weakened heart gave out . . .'

'Your theory is interesting,' I said, lighting my first cigarette of the day. 'But you are forgetting one detail.'

'What?'

'The age of the ghost of course! His physical appearance was that of someone of about forty. According to what Watson tells us in "The Adventure of the Musgrave Ritual", Sherlock Holmes investigated his first case in the 1870s when he was only twenty. So if our man died at forty, we have to put the date of his death at the start of the 1890s. Well! I imagine that you can see that the dates are not compatible! In Conan Doyle's stories, Holmes ends his career in 1914 with the case called "His Last Bow". At that time, our real human bloodhound (if indeed he ever existed!) had kicked the bucket a quarter of a century beforehand!'

'You seem to be ignoring what Dr Dryden himself explained to us when we met for the first time: spirits can use a pre-existing image of themselves to materialise. Maybe this is a stylish ghost who prefers to show himself as he was when he was forty rather than sixty!'

'You really do have an answer for everything this morning, don't you!'

'Not at all! For a start, I cannot establish the link between this ghost and the bloody crimes in the city. Why did he get angry when I asked him about that? And how could he know that another murder would take place tonight in Narrow Street?'

'Well, I suppose we'll have to go and find out.'

'Heavens!' exclaimed James, returning to his place in the middle of the sitting room for another set of exercises. 'Now we just need to decide what to do first today!'

'I don't know about you but I'm going to Victoria Street to find a bookshop. I'm looking for a particular book and I'm sure I'll find it there. Afterwards, well, I think I'll go to the British Museum Reading Room.'

'Andrew, you're not serious!' James was offended, his arms frozen in position in the overheated air of the room. 'Here we are, in the middle of an incredible adventure, and you can't find anything better to do than nose around a bookshop! You really are priceless!'

'Excuse me but it's not just any old bookshop! It's the Psychic Bookshop.[10] The edition of Conan Doyle's work I consulted yesterday had a detailed biography. I saw that in 1925 Arthur opened this shop, dedicated to spiritualism and the occult sciences, and entrusted its management to his daughter, Mary Louise. If your theory concerning the relationship between the writer and his character is correct, we will no doubt find some interesting information in his autobiography, *Memories and Adventures*.'

'Aha! In that case, I'll come with you. Who knows? Maybe Conan Doyle's daughter will be able to shed some light on all this. Just let me change.'

Five minutes later we were standing at the Great Russell Street taxi rank.

'Abbey House on Victoria Street,' I told the driver.

'Is it far?' James asked me.

'The other side of St James's Park, I think. A stone's throw from the Houses of Parliament.'

The cab reached our destination in just quarter of an hour. The bookshop was located at the top of Victoria Street, No. 2, in the shadow of Westminster Abbey. The façade was fairly discreet but inside it was not lacking in charm with its long wooden shelves filled with books. The shop contained everything it was possible to read about spiritualism at that time: works on the Fox sisters from Hydesville in New York State where the movement began in 1848, books by William Crookes, Alfred Russell Wallace, Camille Flammarion, Allan Kardex, Charles Richet, Léon Denis, Gabriel Delanne, Henri Regnault, Dr Geley, Alexandre Aksakof, Colonel de Rochas and many more. And of course, books by the shop's former owner.

Behind the counter a small, rather round dark-haired lady was bustling about jovially, busy preparing a parcel. She must have been about forty-five.

'Do we have the honour of speaking to Mary Louise Conan Doyle?'[11] James asked, approaching the counter.

'I'm Mary,' the lady replied, adding the final touches to her parcel. 'What can I do for you, gentlemen?'

'Let me introduce myself. I am James Trelawney and this is my associate, Andrew Singleton. We are private detectives. Lady Conan Doyle has charged us with investigating the recent psychic events at 221 Baker Street. You have no doubt heard of them?'

'Yes. Jean had already told me of her intention to engage the services of a detective. What made her reluctant was the fear of not being taken seriously. I see that she has found good people – otherwise you would not have ventured into my spiritualist lair. Non-believers are always afraid of coming face to face with a spirit in here.'

'Oh, no ghost could frighten us!' James laughed.

'Were you at Windlesham the night your father died?' I asked.

'No, only Jean and her three children were there. Windlesham was the house my father bought to live in with his new wife and create a new family. I never lived there, you see. But I was always welcomed with open arms.'

Just then I heard the doorbell chime and a small man, almost a dwarf, with a red moustache and a yellow cap, entered the shop. He headed for a shelf of books near the window with a very business-like air.

'Your stepmother no doubt shared her fears as to your father's death,' James resumed. 'According to her, there was apparently a link between it and the phenomena at Number 221. What is your opinion?'

'I admit that I don't really know. The doctor concluded that my father died of a heart attack. He had a weak heart and he had exhausted himself in the last years of his life. There was nothing very mysterious there. As to the phenomena you speak of, it seems that no one knows exactly what is going on. As far as I understand, it would appear to be a simple case of haunting.'

'One thing keeps bothering me,' said James, resting his elbow on the counter and leaning towards Miss Conan Doyle. 'And I hope you can enlighten me. Do you think it possible that Sherlock Holmes really existed?'

Mary Louise Conan Doyle's smiling face became defiant. She hesitated for a moment, sizing us up, and then replied, 'Well, my father never concealed the fact that Holmes owed much to his old professor at the Faculty of Medicine in Edinburgh, Joseph Bell. His keen intelligence and deductive faculties broadly inspired my father's hero. What's more, Sherlock Holmes's first adventures were dedicated to Professor Bell.'

For the last few minutes I had had the persistent and disagreeable impression that we were being watched. I turned my head towards the man with the yellow cap. He appeared to be captivated by our conversation. When he realised that I was looking at him, he immediately turned away and pretended to study a book he was holding in his hands.

'I fear that I haven't made myself clear,' corrected my friend. 'What I meant was, is it possible that Sherlock Holmes was a real person and that this person actually accomplished everything that the hero we know was supposed to have done, and that Arthur Conan Doyle was just the faithful chronicler of his adventures?'

'Oh, I understand! You are one of those thousands of aficionados around the world who truly believe that Holmes is a real person! My father was always surprised to see how much his hero had acquired an independent existence in the hearts of his contemporaries. He also received many letters from men and women requesting Sherlock Holmes's services and asking my father to forward their letters to him. At the risk of disappointing you, you should know that this fictitious character came straight out of Arthur Conan Doyle's brain. His creation is absolutely original. If you have no other questions, gentlemen, please excuse me. I have work to do.'

'About 221 Baker Street,' I cut in, 'we should make clear that it is not just a simple case of haunting. Last night we participated in a séance at that address organised by Dr Dryden from the Society for Psychical Research. And to the amazement of all present, the ghost of Sherlock Holmes materialised!'

Miss Conan Doyle was overcome with laughter.

'But that's impossible!' she said, once she had controlled her hilarity somewhat. 'I can assure you that Holmes does not exist! You were tricked, gentlemen. You have been the victims of a malicious conjuring trick. Sadly, it is not uncommon. Our movement has been invaded by all sorts of illusionists. Honest, staunch spiritualists are doing their best to hunt out the forgers and tricksters. All his life my father fought against people like that. I am not even very surprised that it was the SPR, and Dr Dryden in particular. They always mocked my father and boasted that they were beyond reproach!'

I felt James's frustration rising next to me. Discreetly, I touched his arm to restrain him. It was pointless to insist; we would learn nothing further.

In reality, I was myself a little offended by the reaction of Conan Doyle's eldest child. By categorically denying the existence of a real Sherlock Holmes, she corroborated my initial hunch and I had not expected anything less from her. But by immediately challenging the materialisation of a spirit during the séance at 221 Baker Street, she was also discrediting the appearance of Blanche and therefore the message she had sent me. That was something I could not accept. I had only one desire at that moment: to get away as quickly as possible.

'We have wasted enough of your time,' I said, trying to hide my feelings. 'But before we go, I would like to buy your father's autobiography. I imagine you have it in stock?'

'Just a moment, please.'

Miss Conan Doyle went into the office behind the counter and returned a few minutes later with a copy of *Memories and Adventures*, published by Hodder & Stoughton in 1924.

'A whole chapter is dedicated to the creation of the Sherlock Holmes character,' she said, holding out the book. 'You will find confirmation of everything I have told you.'

'We will read it with great interest, believe me, Miss Conan Doyle.'

I paid and we quickly headed for the exit.

'Sherlock Holmes is a work of fiction, gentlemen!' she thundered. 'His spirit could not possibly have materialised at 221 Baker Street! Do you hear me? *It is categorically impossible!*'

We both remained silent. As we passed the little man (who turned out to be older than he had seemed at first sight, although I could still not fix his age with certainty), he greeted me, touching his cap with his hand. I returned the gesture but reflected that he was staring at me in a very odd way.

Once outside on the pavement, James lost his temper.

'Well, I'll be damned! She took us for a couple of fools, didn't she! I'd like to have seen her face when that ghost appeared!'

'Well, it's not surprising she didn't believe us. And you know, I too am convinced that Sherlock Holmes never existed. That idea does not stand up to analysis. What's more, I may have another clue.'

'Well, if you agree with her too . . . !' said James, stung by the lack of credence I was giving to his theory. 'As to this other idea, may I at least know what it is?'

'Not yet! I must admit that nothing is very clear in my head at the moment.'

'So we are no further on!'

We headed in the direction of the river and after a few minutes arrived at Millbank. The Houses of Parliament looked impressive on the other side of the road.

'Indirectly, we're approaching the scene of last night's crime,' I observed, admiring the architecture of the Palace of Westminster and the famous Victoria Tower. 'Wasn't the victim a member of this eminent institution?'

'He was,' grunted my associate.

'The murder was committed in an alleyway off the Strand. If I am not mistaken, it is a little further on, along the Thames towards Waterloo Bridge. Let's try to find out a bit more about what happened.'

I approached a newspaper seller and bought a copy of the *Spectator*. Its headline read: MEMBER OF PARLIAMENT SAVAGELY MURDERED.

According to the article, a young lady lodging on the top floor of a house which overlooked the alleyway at the back had witnessed the crime as she had been looking out of the window at the time of the attack. She stated that Sir Thomas Blunden was strolling peacefully in the middle of the alleyway, which had been deserted because of the fairly early hour, when suddenly, seemingly from nowhere, a man with an indistinct form and jerky step appeared in front of him. As Sir Thomas passed the stranger, the latter turned, brandished a cane at Blunden's head, shouting, and threw himself on the old gentleman. He had struck him in the face and all over the body with an animal-like rage, so much so that the cane had broken in two. Then he had punched and kicked him repeatedly and stamped on him furiously, breaking his bones into a thousand pieces. When it was clear that the poor man was no longer breathing, the fiend had simply vanished into the dark night.

The details of this obscene crime awoke distant memories from my time as a boarder at Dartmouth. Then I had been a fervent admirer of Robert Louis Stevenson and had read most of his books half a dozen times.

'Curiouser and curiouser!' I said, lifting my head from the

newspaper. 'It seems that the murderer has copied a famous novel again.'

'What do you mean?'

'*The Strange Case of Dr Jekyll and Mr Hyde* by Stevenson. If my memory serves me correctly, the author refers to the murder of Sir Danvers Carew by the dreadful Edward Hyde, Dr Jekyll's Machiavellian twin. The same weapon was used (a cane) with the same brutality, the same dreary and deserted location . . .'

'Mr Hyde, Dorian Gray, Dracula . . . we are drowning in fiction!'

'It can't be a coincidence. The murderer or murderers are delighting in committing crimes dreamt up by Victorians writers. Unless . . .'

'Unless . . . ?' repeated James dubiously.

'Hopefully I will be able to tell you more in a few hours' time! In the meanwhile, I have to go to the British Museum immediately. Let's meet at Montague Street this evening.'

And I leapt onto the omnibus heading for Bloomsbury as my associate looked on, dumbfounded.

X

A LITTLE READING NEVER HURT ANYONE

I SPENT the rest of the day under the immense dome of the Reading Room. It was Saturday and the Museum was very busy. By chance my favourite spot (C4) was empty and, twenty minutes after I arrived, I was installed with a raft of books by Arthur Conan Doyle in front of me which I hoped, with a bit of luck, could clarify our case. Amongst other things my table held *The History of Spiritualism, The Vital Message, The Land of Mist* – a short novel inspired by spiritualism published in 1926 – as well as two collections of fantasy stories published in 1922, a large number of which borrowed from spiritualist theories.

In the first instance, I was looking for information on Sir Arthur's life. No biography of the writer had yet been written at that time so I had to make do with what I could find.

I had a number of magazines in which Conan Doyle had published articles and interviews, particularly back issues of *Light*, and my volume of memoirs purchased at the Psychic Bookshop. Not having any paper to write on, I used the inside cover of the autobiography to make notes on what I found. I then settled down to consulting the books and magazines in search of any clues, however small, which might indicate the relationship the writer had had with his character. I was certain that this was one of the essential elements of the affair.

From the mass of information collected that afternoon, here is what I was able to establish once everything had been put in order.

1. ON THE WRITER/CHARACTER RELATIONSHIP

Conan Doyle created Sherlock Holmes in spring 1886 in a short novel called *A Study in Scarlet*, at the start of which he described in detail the meeting between the narrator (our dear Dr Watson) and the detective, then about to embark on his illustrious career. At the time, Conan Doyle was himself a young doctor of twenty-seven, recently arrived in Southsea, a suburb of Portsmouth. He had had a few short stories published in magazines and had completed his first historical novel, *The Firm of Girdlestone*, two years earlier. It was only published in 1890. *A Study in Scarlet* did not have to wait so long. A few months after it was completed, and despite being rejected by a few publishers, the novel appeared in *Beeton's Christmas Annual* in December 1887 and subsequently in a book published by Ward, Lock & Co. in 1888.

Having barely finished *A Study in Scarlet*, Conan Doyle launched himself into writing a new historical novel, *Micah Clarke*, which was published in 1889 to great acclaim. It is interesting that for Arthur Conan Doyle the many historical novels he published throughout his career were the noble part of his work, the part to which he gave all his energy, and he would have liked to see them more widely recognised. Instead, it has to be said, it was what he considered to be the commercial element of his work, the Sherlock Holmes stories, which brought him the greatest recognition.

In 1889 he had to interrupt the writing of a new historical novel to go to London at the invitation of the editor of a literary magazine based in Philadelphia, *Lippincott's Magazine*, who was actively seeking new talent. As well as Arthur Conan Doyle, another young British writer, Oscar Wilde, was invited to the dinner. Thanks to a good meal where the wine flowed, John Stoddart, the magazine's editor, managed to confirm orders for a new novel from his two guests to be serialised in *Lippincott's* the following year. Wilde wrote *The Picture of Dorian Gray*; Conan Doyle wrote *The Sign of Four* in which he put his detective in the saddle for his second and, he hoped, last case.

He had not reckoned with the novel becoming such a success with British and American readers, particularly the character of the infallible human bloodhound. Consequently, in 1890 the *Strand Magazine* requested that the author write a series of short stories with the promise of simultaneous publication in London and New York. The contract was also very lucrative. Conan Doyle had recently moved to London and had decided to abandon medicine to devote himself fully to writing. Under those circumstances, it was difficult to turn up his nose. 'A Scandal in Bohemia' was therefore published in July 1891, followed by eleven other stories. The success was incredible. Each issue sold like hot cakes, with people queuing up as soon as the newspaper kiosks opened so as not to miss it. Within a few months, Arthur Conan Doyle had become famous across the world. But the other side of success was that the writer was now just the 'father of Sherlock Holmes'. Out went his historical work – no one wanted it.

The situation became even more irksome as people began to amuse themselves by pretending that Sherlock Holmes was a real person (or did they really believe it?). Letters from readers were full of justifications of the theory, and articles and stories appeared apparently telling of the hero's adventures. There were also letters addressed to the magazine and the author requesting the detective's services. The name of Sherlock Holmes was everywhere, in everyone's minds and on everyone's lips.

In 1892, succumbing to financial necessity, Conan Doyle agreed to write eleven new stories. However, the following year, realising that he had become a prisoner of his character, he took a difficult but, he believed, wise decision: he would kill off Sherlock Holmes. In December 1893, at the end of 'The Final Problem', readers were dismayed to learn that their hero had fallen to his death during mortal combat at Reichenbach Falls in Switzerland, accompanied by his sworn enemy, Professor Moriarty, the 'Napoleon of Crime'.

Conan Doyle was very satisfied with this ending and told himself that he would never hear another word about Sherlock Holmes.

Freed from his hero's stranglehold, the writer dedicated himself to his historical novels, travelled to Egypt, served in a hospital in Bloemfontein during the Boer War, threw himself into politics in Edinburgh (his home town) and was knighted by the King in 1902. Conan Doyle felt like a new man, enjoying the pleasure of being free once more. He had also met the beautiful young Jean Leckie and, although their love remained platonic, his heart, too, was rejuvenated. In 1901 he even agreed to go some way towards satisfying the public, who had continued to demand the return of their favourite detective, by publishing a new Sherlock Holmes adventure, *The Hound of the Baskervilles*.

As the events in the novel were supposed to have taken place before the hero's death, Conan Doyle's honour was safe. Readers therefore rushed to the kiosks again to buy copies of the *Strand*.

But had Arthur Conan Doyle innocently opened Pandora's box? Sam McClure, editor of the American weekly *Collier's*, immediately offered an incredible amount of money in exchange for the detective's return. But not a pretend return as in *The Hound of the Baskervilles*. No, the author must strive to bring his hero safely out of Reichenbach Falls and announce to the whole world that he really was back.

For Arthur Conan Doyle the calculation did not take long: he had had no literary success since his last collection of Holmes stories; the time and money devoted to public affairs, particularly his unsuccessful attempts to enter politics, had left him penniless and his creative energy considerably dissipated. The public was dying to read more adventures of the Baker Street sleuth. Mary Doyle, his mother and greatest admirer, who had been fiercely opposed to the 'murder' of Sherlock Holmes ten years earlier, asked him every day to bring Holmes back to life.

Conan Doyle eventually brought him back in 1903 in a short story called 'The Adventure of the Empty House'. He wrote thirty-three stories, including one novel, until March 1927 when 'The Adventure of Shoscombe Old Place', published in *Liberty Magazine*, finally ended his literary output.

2. THE MYSTERIOUS DR BROWN

Of all the books I scrutinised that day, as I sat enthralled at my table, unaware of everything around me in the Reading Room, it was Sir Arthur's autobiography that provided the most interesting information: in 1898, before moving to Windlesham, he had been living in a large house called Undershaw in Hindhead, Surrey. Conan Doyle's neighbour was a country doctor whose name he preferred not to reveal and whom he called simply Dr Brown. This Brown, who was very small in stature, was involved in occultism and one day suggested that Conan Doyle join a secret society. When asked what the result would be if he joined, Brown told Doyle that he would acquire supernatural powers. When asked what he would have to do once part of this organisation, Brown replied that he would have to study a large number of subjects which were not to be found in printed books but in carefully numbered secret manuscripts entrusted to the initiated as a sign of privilege and duty. Conan Doyle was greatly interested and gave the strange country doctor his agreement.

Shortly afterwards, the writer was awakened by convulsions passing through his entire body like strong electric tremors. He immediately wondered if the doctor had had anything to do with this unpleasant experience. A few days later he received another visit from Dr Brown, who told him that he could now join the organisation. Conan Doyle was suddenly terrified of the consequences of such a commitment and rejected the invitation, saying that his life was too busy and would not give him time to devote himself to the new task.

After a couple of weeks Dr Brown came back to see the writer, accompanied by one of his associates. Intrigued, Conan Doyle listened as the two visitors spoke of the marvels they had seen and had themselves actually accomplished, such as out-of-body experiences.

Conan Doyle ended his peculiar tale by adding that he had seen Dr Brown again in 1923 in Portland, Oregon, at one of his spiritualist lectures. He supposed that the brotherhood to which the little man belonged was a sort of Rosicrucian sect.

3. WHEN CONAN DOYLE DISCOVERED SPIRITUALIST THEORIES

I then consulted an interview published in the spiritualist magazine *Light* in 1919, which proved to be enlightening. I was surprised to learn that the first table-turning séance in which the writer had participated actually dated back to the end of 1886. His interest in spiritualism had begun very early on and in any case well before 1916. Conan Doyle subsequently continued to frequent the circles of disciples. It might therefore be deduced that he was already convinced of the existence of a psychic realm when he committed what might be called literary suicide by killing off Sherlock Holmes at Reichenbach Falls.

4. ALL THOUGHTS ARE THINGS

Finally, I was extremely disconcerted by a short story called 'Playing with Fire' in which Arthur Conan Doyle described what happened during a spiritualist séance organised in an artist's studio. That evening the meeting had almost turned into a nightmare after one of the guests put forward the theory that thoughts were things and that by imagining something, one actually gave it form. As the occupant of the studio had spent the day working on the painting of a unicorn, the group tested the theory by trying to invoke the animal's spirit. The experiment surpassed all expectation because not only did the unicorn materialise most impressively, but it also wrecked the entire room, almost impaling one of the guests on its white horn.

Mental images taking form! Thoughts coming alive! What was I to make of this magical story written at the end of the 1890s, just before Sherlock Holmes was resurrected? The parallels with the events that interested us were striking. Was it possible that the character invented by Conan Doyle had somehow taken on a living form, that he had begun to enjoy an autonomous existence, independent of his creator? The theory was truly incredible and unlikely, but it did shed unexpected light on the series of murders committed over the last few months in London. If our favourite detective could penetrate our reality, there was nothing to prevent other fictitious characters, much less respectable creatures, from doing the same.

As for this obscure Dr Brown, was it possible to find out where he was today, in 1932? Perhaps Lady Conan Doyle could give us some information.

A literary crime . . . supernatural powers . . . spiritualist séances going wrong. Whatever the truth, I was now convinced that they were connected.

I was lost in these frenzied speculations when the bell announced that the Museum was closing. I quickly left the Reading Room, crossed the monumental portico which never failed to move me deeply whenever I passed through it, and left the building, my brain and my nerves electrified by what I had learnt but highly satisfied with the results.

I returned to our rooms in Montague Street with my book,

now covered in notes, under my arm and found James pacing up and down the sitting room.

'Would it be indiscreet to ask what on earth you have been doing?' he asked as I hurried to the telephone.

'First, I have an urgent question for our visitor . . .' I replied, searching in my jacket pockets. With Lady Conan Doyle's card in my hand, I dialled the number of Windlesham. The property was located in Crowborough, Sussex, about two hours from the capital by train.

At the end of the line the telephone rang several times. Finally, it was answered and I heard a male voice. It was the butler. Lady Conan Doyle was not at Windlesham and she would not return before the evening.

'Could you please inform her that Mr Singleton and Mr Trelawney need to see her as soon as possible and that they would like her to come to Montague Street tomorrow morning at 10 a.m. Singleton and Trelawney – have you made a note of the names? It is extremely important. Thank you.'

I hung up.

'Why have you done that?' asked my associate with a touch of irritation. My actions appeared entirely illogical to him (and I must admit that this was an unfailing source of amusement to me!).

'I learnt something extremely interesting at the British Museum! I think that we are getting closer to understanding this mystery.'

'May I ask what it's all about?'

'First I need confirmation – but it shouldn't take long.'

'And the truth came from dusty old manuscripts? Bah!

That's not how we'll solve this case. Muscles will be much more useful tonight at Narrow Street when we try to stop this great dangerous, bloodthirsty brute from harming anyone else!'

XI

A NIGHT IN THE EAST END

IT was just after 11.30 p.m. when the taxi dropped us off at Commercial Road near Bromley Street. It was the first time in three months of living in the capital that we had ventured so far from the centre. Until now, our peregrinations towards the East End had been idly limited to Houndsditch and Bishopsgate. Going beyond Aldgate and heading in the direction of Whitechapel High Street and Commercial Road, we were surprised to discover another world: sombre, poverty-stricken, fascinating and frozen in time for nearly two hundred years. Apart from the few cars which were still passing at this late hour, there was nothing to show with certainty that it was 1932. Small streetlamps spaced too far apart only partially lit the street, leaving long stretches of darkness to fester between them where a legion of demons could have been crouching without risk of being seen.

So this was where millions of London's poor lived, the people the rich had chased from the nice areas in the west and centre over time. In Whitechapel and Limehouse the lucky ones worked hard to pay for their lodgings and feed their families. As for the others, most of them lived by their wits; they begged, they went on the game, they robbed their neighbours, and above all they drank crude wine and cheap spirits until they were out of their minds, in order to try to forget a life of destitution without pleasure or love.

It was in these streets that Jack the Ripper had committed a series of crimes that had gone unpunished.

And here, forty-four years later, the good people of Whitechapel were reliving the same nightmare. It was as if bad luck did not want to loosen its grip on such easy prey.

We stood for a few minutes without moving in front of this spectacle of a world out of time, tormented by a past of blood and pain. We did not know where to go. James was the first to break the silence.

'Ratcliffe Street,' he said, pointing to a small dark street leading towards the Thames. 'I think it's that way. If I remember rightly, according to our map Narrow Street is further down, near the river.'

The name Ratcliffe brought back a flood of memories from my reading. In *On Murder Considered as One of the Fine Arts*, Thomas De Quincey had given a lengthy description of Ratcliffe Highway where a terrible murder had taken place in the winter of 1812 (two generations before the abominations of Jack the Ripper), which had left its mark on the memory of the inhabitants of the East End for ever. John Williams, a crazy, savage but meticulous killer who had obviously had some practice, entered the home of the Marr family in the middle of the night and massacred them in the space of a few minutes.

There was no doubt about it. James and I were standing at one of the entrances to hell.

As we approached the docks, the air became imbued with the stench of seaweed and the tide. We wandered down a succession of alleyways, each more lugubrious and badly lit than the one before, eventually reaching Narrow Street ten minutes later.

I did not think much of the area and, deep down, I began to regret walking into such a trap. It was one thing to construct wild theories in the cosy comfort of a sitting room or the marble silence of a Reading Room but a dark and windy street in the middle of the night was quite another matter.

James thought we should begin exploring immediately. His eyes were shining and his step was brisk. He was a man of action and he relished the palpable tension in this bleak, possibly murderous setting.

Narrow Street followed the Thames. For the first thirty yards it was particularly narrow and then it suddenly widened as it forked sharply right and there was slightly more light. Halfway along, it crossed Regent's Canal, which served to relieve the pressure on the river wharfs, enabling smaller vessels to drop anchor in Limehouse Basin, the lanterns of which we saw swaying in the shadows on our left. The street then continued for about three hundred yards to the junction with Ropemakers Fields and Fore Street.

From time to time access to the docks on our right created sudden gaps and, under London's smoggy sky, we glimpsed an unlikely mix of masts and chimneys belonging to the numerous brigs, clippers, schooners and steamers moored on the loop of the river for the night.

It was obvious that the street was little used. The number of people we met could be counted on the fingers of one hand. Once, at the door of a tavern, an innkeeper forcibly ejected a drunkard. He fell into the gutter, got up, shouting abuse at the man who had treated him so harshly, and then went to sprawl in a corner on the other side of the street, no doubt to sleep it off until daybreak. On another occasion, a man knocked at the door of one of the seamen's lodgings that abounded in the area. We vaguely heard a few words being exchanged through a window and then the door opened and he entered the establishment. Further on still, we met two sailors. Hearing them speak, I supposed that they were Swedish or Finnish. And that was essentially it.

At midnight, we had finished our explorations. Now we had to agree on a strategy, which would not be easy because of the layout of the area.

'The street must be about six hundred yards long,' said James when we reached the junction. 'If the killer puts in an appearance at one end of the street while we're at the other we'll have wasted our time. We'd better split up. I suggest you take the first half from Ratcliffe Cross to the canal and I'll take the second, from the canal to here. That way we'll halve the risk of missing him.'

'Your suggestion does appear sensible at first glance,' I replied, suddenly alarmed at the idea of finding myself alone, 'but, actually, I think it would be wiser to stay together . . .'

'Good heavens, you're frightened!' James exclaimed with a smile which was a shade mocking. 'Don't worry. If you're in danger just shout as loud as you can and I'll do the same if I need help. In this wilderness it would be incredible if we didn't hear one another.'

We retraced our steps and stopped at the canal. Beneath our feet we heard the lapping of the dirty viscous water but the weak light from the streetlamps meant that we could not see beyond the parapets.

'We should go now, each to our end. Let's meet here in quarter of an hour. The first to arrive should wait for the other. Keep alert and please try not to cry out if a black cat crosses your path.'

Without further delay, having reeled off his litany of instructions, he headed east. I suspected that he had not appreciated my doubts as to his theory on the existence of Sherlock Holmes. The strapping fellow was decidedly sensitive and I vowed to take that into consideration in future.

Meanwhile, I did not have much choice. I put my cigarette holder between my lips and headed back the way we had come, my hands in my trouser pockets and the collar of my jacket turned up to help shield me from the chill of the night.

I did not meet a living soul along the route. But when I reached the part where the street narrowed so as to form a dark passage, I heard noises coming from the direction I was headed. I immediately threw away my cigarette and stood against the wall that was set back from the path. I waited for a few seconds, holding my breath. A shadow slipped past me and continued on its way with a resolute air. The man was wearing a black coat and a cap, both of which had seen better days. In all probability, it was another sailor looking for a bed for the night. After letting him get ahead, I carefully followed him. The man continued for about fifty yards and then, as I had expected, knocked at the door of a boarding house called the Yellow Dragon. I hid in the shadows while he showed his credentials and was ushered inside the house. Then I returned to the path.

James was already waiting for me by the canal.

'Did you see anything?'

'Nothing significant,' I replied, lighting another cigarette. 'Just a sailor looking for lodgings. Otherwise, it was very quiet.'

'I didn't do much better. I met an old prostitute who turned into Globe Alley and a stray dog who stuck to me like glue the whole way. Fortunately, he gave up in the end. Right, it's only half past midnight. We should keep going!'

We each set off to our respective ends once more. Again, I walked to the passage without meeting anyone. After watching for a few minutes, I hurried back in the direction of the canal where this time I arrived first.

Just after I arrived I noticed two figures coming towards me from the part of the street James was supposed to be checking. I did not have time to conceal myself. I turned towards the basin and leant over the rusty parapet. The footsteps were getting closer. I could make out a male voice with a strong Irish accent and female laughter. I surreptitiously turned my gaze in their direction and saw their faces. He was a sailor with the sunburnt face of someone who spends their life travelling under sun-drenched skies; she was a prostitute, about thirty, with a rather pretty face. They were walking arm in arm and seemed to be in good humour. Passing behind me, the man dropped his voice but I heard him say a few words: 'port of call', 'beer', 'Borneo'. Eventually, the couple disappeared at the other end of the street.

But there was still no sign of my companion.

I waited for a little while and then, in desperation, decided to go and look for him.

With every passing second I realised more and more acutely

how foolish we had been in organising this expedition. It would have been wiser to warn Scotland Yard. After all, several leading figures had been present at that séance and, like us, they had heard the ghost's advice to James. Even if spiritualist theories were not viewed positively at the Yard, an inspector would surely have taken the time to check what we were saying. Now it was too late to withdraw.

I walked for a long time without seeing anything at all. Then suddenly, as I passed one of the stairways which led down to the wharfs, I thought I heard a noise, a sort of muffled groan. I stopped dead and leant over the steps. I could not see much because of the darkness but it was clear that, below me, someone was going down onto the wharf.

'James!' I called softly, not at all sure that it was my associate.

That was when a huge hand covered my mouth. My heart skipped a beat and I was thrown back against the wall. In the space of an instant I believed that my time had come to say goodbye to this world.

'You fool!' whispered my friend's voice. 'You almost gave us away.'

'You scared me half to death! I heard a noise at the bottom of those stairs. I thought it was you . . .'

'It's our man, I'm sure of it. I've been following him at a good distance for ten minutes. He's wearing a long black coat, an old-fashioned top hat and was threatening a woman he has with him.'

'Were you able to see his face?'

'No, I hid in the corner of an alleyway when they passed me.

All I can say is that the poor girl is worried sick. He's gagged her so she can't cry out. Once she tried to get away and he broke her arm with a single blow. I heard the crack! It still makes me shiver.'

'We have to do something,' I murmured, panicking. 'I'll run and get the police.'

'They'll never get here in time. No, the only solution is to intervene ourselves.'

'But we might be killed!'

'Not with this!'

James took a revolver from his pocket and the metal shone in the moonlight.

'Are you out of your mind? That will only make things worse!'

'On the contrary, it will be very useful. I'll go first. There isn't a moment to lose. And don't make a sound.'

I did not have time to reply. James had already started down the first step.

To tell the truth, I no longer knew what to do. Faced with this situation, I was paralysed with fear and it was only because I had no choice that I fell in behind him robotically, without thinking for a moment about what might happen.

It was damp and the steps were slippery. Several times I almost fell. Yet, somehow or other, we made it down to the wharf.

At the bottom of the steps James suddenly stopped and I hit my forehead on his shoulder.

'Look!' he said in my ear.

In front of us, about twenty yards away at the end of the

wharf, a large black shadow was sitting astride what seemed to be the body of a young woman. She was trying to put up a struggle but the superhuman strength of her assailant was preventing her from throwing him off. He had just taken out a dagger, or perhaps a long scalpel. He held it in his right hand, the sharp blade over the victim's face. We could clearly hear her moans of terror.

'That's him! That's our killer!' I heard myself say.

'Hey! Don't move or I'll shoot!' shouted James, pointing his revolver in the attacker's direction.

The figure was not expecting to be disturbed. He immediately leapt up, roaring like an enraged animal and brandishing his blade at us. At that distance and without any light we could not see what he looked like. But just at that moment the lanterns of a large vessel sliding past in the direction of Wapping shed a little light on the end of the wharf – enough in any case to see that where there should have been a face underneath the slightly turned-down hat and between the open sides of his coat was a milky, glutinous substance, a luminescent nothingness for a body.

'Well, I'll be damned!' exclaimed my associate in alarm. 'That's not a man – it's a ghost!'

My theory had been brilliantly confirmed but I would have given a lot at that moment for it to have been otherwise! The situation was critical and only one question needed to be answered: what were we going to do to get out of this? I admit that neither James nor I had the slightest idea.

'Drop the gun!' I begged. James was still pointing his revolver in the direction of the ghost. 'There's no point shooting him. It might make him worse!'

But it was too late; we had unleashed his fury. The shadow hit his victim with exceptional force and then rushed at us, the autopsy knife raised, ready to cut us as soon as we were within reach.

Footsteps could be heard on the steps behind us. Hopefully, it was allies and not more fantastic creatures who would take us from behind.

The killer was only thirty feet away.

We instinctively recoiled as our adversary advanced. Suddenly, James's heel became caught in a hole in the ground. He stumbled and fell violently backwards. His head hit the bottom step and the jolt caused him to pull the trigger. The bullet hit the black coat in the stomach. As expected, the only effect was to seal our fate even faster. James slid into unconsciousness on the ground and I was frozen with fright. That would have been the end of us if a voice had not suddenly cried out, 'By Elohim, leave this place, evil spirit, and return to the darkness!'

Incredibly, the command, made in a firm voice and with amazing calm, had an almost instant effect. The ghost panicked and let the scalpel fall to the ground. Suddenly, when he was only a few feet from us, he disappeared into the dark night like a wisp of mist.

You can imagine my surprise when I recognised our saviour as the little man in the yellow cap whom we had met earlier at the bookshop. He came down the last of the steps, returning one of those big Yankee daggers called bowie knives to its sheath, hidden inside the left-hand side of his jacket. Now he leant over my friend.

'His fall has knocked him out,' the little man said, examining his head. 'His scalp is bleeding a little but he's strong; he's going to be fine.'

He then got up to check on the young woman at the end of the wharf and make sure that she too was fine. I contented myself with following him, without saying a word. At his request, I helped him undo the strip of material the attacker had stuck in the victim's mouth, my fingers still trembling. He took her pulse.

'She's unconscious but her life is not in danger, thank goodness.'

'Whoever you are, thank you! Without you we would just be three miserable bodies whose deaths would be the subject of the evening editions.'

'Most probably,' he replied in an unruffled voice that was totally at odds with the trembling which continued to affect my entire body.

'May I ask to whom I have the honour of speaking?'

'My name is Kirkby, Dr Ashley Kirkby. If you have had the time to glance at your copy of Conan Doyle's memoirs, I should be known to you. Sir Arthur was kind enough to devote three pages to me. He used a pseudonym though.'

'Dr Brown! That's you?'

'Well deduced, young man!'

'So you have been following us all day then, Dr Kirkby?'

'And thank goodness I did! It was Dr John Dryden who persuaded me. He brought me up to date with what happened at the séance yesterday. He also told me of the message given to you by Mr Holmes's ghost. Dryden was very worried about you. I was rather surprised that he contacted me but he is an excellent chap deep down, who is better than his awkward manner might suggest. But his total lack of open-mindedness regarding the invisible world is very sad. Of course, he is not alone. The entire spiritualist movement's vision is far too narrow.'

'In any event, I will thank him, I assure you.'

'I think we should take this young lady to the London Hospital quickly,' he said, turning his attention to the young woman once more. 'My car is not far away. I will take her. Wait here. I will send someone to help your friend.'

The little man in the yellow cap, who could not have been more than four foot nine (and was approaching his sixty-ninth birthday, as he confided to me a few weeks later) immediately lifted the body of the young woman with disconcerting ease. I remembered the long list of alleged powers that Conan Doyle had attributed to the doctor in his autobiography. Did he really belong to that occult brotherhood?

'I have an appointment with Lady Conan Doyle at our rooms in Montague Street,' I said to the mysterious little man, accompanying him to the bottom of the steps. 'Tomorrow morning at ten o'clock. Can you believe, I meant to ask her about Dr Brown! And also give her my initial conclusions about the case.'

'That's perfect. I'll be there with Dr Dryden. You will be able to present your results to a larger audience. I'm dying to hear them and compare them with my own. I think we'll need several brains to solve this mystery! As for what Lady Conan Doyle could have told you about me, I fear that you would have been disappointed. We met briefly at a conference in the United States attended by her husband. And I am sure that I was far from being the subject of their discussions. See you tomorrow!'

Despite his burden, the little man mounted the stone steps lightly.

'Dr Kirkby!' I called before he had completely disappeared into the darkness. 'That thing which almost cut our throats, do you think it could have been . . . ?'

'Without a shadow of a doubt,' he said. 'Well, to be precise let us say his disembodied spirit!'

XII

WE LEARN WHY AND HOW

THE following day, Sunday 26 June 1932, Lady Conan Doyle was the first to arrive at our lodgings.

'Parker gave me your message,' she said breathlessly as I opened our door. Her cheeks were a little red. 'What have you discovered, Mr Singleton?'

'Well, Lady Conan Doyle, I can go some way to explaining what has been happening – in broad outline at least. Some elements are still unclear but I am counting on the expertise of our next guest, who should be here any minute, to enlighten us.'

'And this next guest is?'

'His name is Ashley Kirkby but your husband called him Dr Brown. He met Dr Kirkby in 1898 and his personality made a great impression on him, to say the least. You met him yourself at a conference in Portland, nine years ago.'

'I'm sorry, I have no memory of it. Oh dear, Mr Trelawney, have you had an accident? Nothing serious, I hope?'

James was a strong, healthy sort of chap and had suffered no more than an impressive cut at the base of his skull. Miss Sigwarth had been very concerned and had insisted that her lodger be examined. The doctor she had called had created a masterpiece of bandaging worthy of Art Deco.

'Thank you for your concern,' James replied. 'I was injured

last night while Andrew and I were trying to prevent the killer who has been the talk of the town recently from committing another crime. And he proved to be . . . well . . . rather special! Fortunately, the cut is superficial. We owe our lives to the impromptu arrival of Dr Kirkby. Thank heavens he came when he did! Without him, that evil phantom—'

'A phantom did you say?'

'I hope that in a few moments,' I said, hearing a knock at the front door, 'we will be able to explain everything.'

A moment later our landlady was showing Dr John Dryden and Dr Ashley Kirkby into our rooms. The latter was still wearing his ubiquitous yellow cap.

'My respects, Lady Conan Doyle,' said Dr Dryden, bowing before the author's widow. 'It has been a long time since I have had the pleasure of seeing you.'

'Dr Dryden!' she replied, revealing a slight irritation. 'I had no idea you were invited to this meeting.'

'Dr Dryden was the one who alerted Dr Kirkby,' I intervened. 'Without him, we would no longer be around to talk to you about this matter. Doctor, on behalf of James and myself I would like to express our profound gratitude.'

'Yes, yes! Kirkby explained briefly this morning,' said Dr Dryden, his tiny eyes shining with satisfaction behind his spectacles. 'After the results of the spiritualist séance, I immediately decided to inform my colleague. Admittedly, he and I have always had a radically different point of view on the nature and motivations of the psychic beings that surround us. At the SPR we support logic and rationality. That is far from being the case amongst Dr Kirkby's friends. That is why they often accuse us of being blind to certain terrible realities of the spirit world because of our overly orthodox view of the spiritualist faith. In my view, Kirkby supports theories that are worthy of great criticism in very many respects. But, well, it is clear that the appearance of Sherlock Holmes's ghost was beyond my understanding!'

'Gentlemen,' I cut in, seeing that the conversation was already taking a very political turn, 'do not forget that this good lady is in the dark as to the latest events. And it would perhaps be helpful for you to know why Lady Conan Doyle came to ask for our assistance. James and I will explain it to you, as well as my inner conviction as regards these mysterious murders committed in London. Then together we must decide what is to be done. But please do sit down.'

Lady Conan Doyle and Dr Dryden sat on the sofa. I let Dr Kirkby and James take the armchairs. I brought a chair over from the dining table and sat next to our female guest.

I suggested that James begin and saw that he was grateful. My friend told of Lady Conan Doyle's visit. He went over the circumstances of Sir Arthur's death, the voice which had been heard on several occasions in the dying man's room, the note written in his hand as he died, the supposed link Lady Conan Doyle had established between that death and the strange phenomena occurring at 221 Baker Street, and the terrible premonition she had had about the murders in London. Then it was my turn. I described our first meeting with Dr Dryden in detail, the photography session in the first-floor sitting room, the spiritualist séance organised a few hours later, the appearance of Sherlock Holmes's ghost, and all the rest right up to our nocturnal expedition to Limehouse and our meeting with the bizarre killer, which had almost been fatal for both of us.

I left nothing out, not even our first disagreeable impressions of Dr Dryden and my conviction that we had been tricked by his psychograph, something that caused Ashley Kirkby great mirth but only effected a tight-lipped smile from Dryden. I also admitted my negative preconceptions of spiritualist theories at the beginning of the case, faithfully described in a few sentences the complexity of my relationship with my father and revealed to Lady Conan Doyle my disappointment as regards certain views she had held during her first visit to us. Finally, I explained how much the psychic séance at 221 Baker Street had shaken my beliefs and changed how I understood the invisible world.

The only thing I suppressed were Blanche's words to me at the séance. I cannot explain this reticence. Perhaps I still felt deep down that this was all somewhat unreal. And if the theory I was preparing to present to these honest people proved to be false, or if I suddenly awoke from the dream in which I had been plunged for two days, there was one thing I wanted to preserve at all costs: the possibility of contacting Leonor Singleton.

'Well!' exclaimed Dr Dryden, having recovered his usual good humour. 'No one can say you refuse to admit your mistakes, young man. For someone who completely rejected the existence of psychic beings, it did not take you long to change your position. If only all non-believers had your open-mindedness! But look here, can you now tell us who, in your opinion, the mysterious phantom was whose criminal activity you opportunely interrupted? I could get nothing out of Dr Kirkby in this respect.'

'Well,' I replied, clearing my throat and glancing at the man in the yellow cap, 'I think that Dr Kirkby will not contradict me if I say that it was the spirit of Jack the Ripper.'

'JACK THE RIPPER?' repeated Dr Dryden, his eyes bulging. 'This is becoming completely incomprehensible! Were you able to see his face then?'

'Yes! Well, no!' James cut in. 'His face had no human features. It was just a kind of big white phosphorescent ball.'

'In that case, how can you be sure that it was the ghost of Jack the Ripper?' asked Lady Conan Doyle.

'Because actually,' I replied, 'I had already come to that conclusion before our terrifying encounter. When you first visited us, Lady Conan Doyle, my attention was drawn to the fact that some of the murders committed over the last few months in the East End were replicas of those committed by Jack the Ripper in 1888. Of course, it could have been the work of a flesh-and-blood individual who found it amusing to replay the same tragedy and that is what we, James and I, had decided. But the article in yesterday's *Daily Gazette* on the murder which occurred at Mitre Square contained one essential detail: a witness who had seen the killer described him as "a kind of shapeless, bloodless, vaporous monster". The fact that the poor man was violently knocked out and lost consciousness just afterwards was not, in my opinion, sufficient to discredit his views, as the journalist writing the article had promptly done. Oh! I admit that, before last night, I for one had a lot of difficulty in persuading myself that the hypothesis of a ghost was an entirely serious one. So much so that, once it was established that the other crimes perpetrated in London over the last few months were all reproductions of crimes described in famous novels, I was not yet prepared to exclude the possibility of a hoax carried out by a fan of Victorian literature.'

'Crimes from famous novels? Victorian literature? For goodness' sake, what are you saying?' asked Dr Dryden.

'The murder of the MP Thomas Blunden on Friday evening,' I resumed, 'was a perfect reproduction of the murder of Sir Danvers Carew as described by Stevenson in *The Strange Case of Dr Jekyll and Mr Hyde*. The murder and mutilation of a prostitute in one of the rooms rented by a certain Miss Farraday in Soho also recall the crimes of the abominable Hyde. But that's not all. In January, bodies were found drained of their blood in Green Park, Bermondsey and Mile End Town. I immediately made the connection with Bram Stoker's novel *Dracula*. Those places are mentioned on several occasions. Finally, another murder was committed this winter in Grosvenor Square, a faithful copy of the one described by Oscar Wilde in *The Picture of Dorian Gray*.'

'Stevenson, Oscar Wilde, Bram Stoker, Conan Doyle,' listed Dr Dryden incredulously. 'We're in a novel, my friends!'

'That is essentially what James said when I set out the similarities between the real crimes and those of fiction. I admit that I myself did not immediately take my theory to its most extreme logical conclusion.'

'And what is that conclusion, Mr Singleton?' asked Lady Conan Doyle.

'It was you, Lady Conan Doyle, who warned us from the beginning of the tragic and unbelievable character of all these events. You spoke of an "unprecedented tragedy, a tragedy no one is ready to confront". Well, you were right!'

'Stop beating about the bush and tell us what this good lady actually thought!' exclaimed Dr Dryden impatiently.

'That London had been invaded by the most terrible band of creatures imaginable! The ghosts of literary monsters created by writers at the end of the last century. Dr Dryden, you would agree, I imagine, that we were all in the presence of the spirit of Sherlock Holmes the other evening at 221 Baker Street? Well, you should know that as we speak somewhere in this city the ghosts of Mr Hyde, Dracula, Dorian Gray *et al.* are hiding. And maybe others still! Ready to strike whenever the fancy takes them!'

'How the devil is that possible?' cried Dr Dryden, his eyes as round as the frames of his spectacles.

'There is a theory on which Dr Kirkby can, I hope, shed some light. Arthur Conan Doyle was assuredly aware of this theory because he used it in one of his stories. It rests on the idea that all human thoughts are things. The more powerful the thought is and the more it comes from a strong, living spirit, the more it is alive, able to lead an autonomous existence in the psychic world. So literary creation is a bit like a sort of factory generating parallel realities.'

'Do you mean to say that when my husband created his character, Sherlock Holmes began to lead an independent life in an undetermined location?'

'Absolutely!' replied Ashley Kirkby who had, until then, remained detached from the conversation. 'And in a place which is not so far away. It is the same one used by the spirits of our dearly departed loved ones. Some eminent writers have spoken of this theory. Lord Bulwer-Lytton, for example, believed that all thoughts have a soul. From the moment a fictitious being is given intellectual energy by its readers, it grows stronger. In the case in point, Lady Conan Doyle, one might say that your husband created one of the most exceptional creatures ever. The fact that millions of men and women around the world are still passionate about his adventures today continues to breathe unequalled psychic intensity into the great hero. Those who innocently believe that he really exists are actually not that far from the truth, although they don't know it . . .'

'Bah!' cried Dr Dryden. 'I know all these occultist theories, Kirkby. But it's nonsense! Nothing has ever been proved.'

'That is where you are wrong, Dryden, as is so often the case. The French have shown themselves to be much more perceptive than us in this instance! The Institut Métaphysique in Paris has carried out all kinds of experiments which have led to insights that you would be well advised not to ignore. It is time to open your eyes, my dear colleague. The invisible world is not peopled only with the poor solitary spirits of our loved ones, it is swarming with elemental spirits, pernicious shadows, abject spectres and hobgoblins for which we are only just beginning to establish a vast catalogue.'

'I have a question for you, Dr Kirkby,' I said to bring an end to these professional squabbles and return to the heart of our problem. 'What made the spirit of Holmes venture into our world?'

'Normally, these beings do not have sufficient psychic density on their own to make themselves visible. But, of course, that does not mean that it is impossible! All I can say is that in this case the renumbering of Baker Street and the allocation of

Number 221 to Major Hipwood's house seem to have played an important role. It is as if the fact that this fictitious address had suddenly become real, and been duly recorded in the land registry of our own world, made it possible for Sherlock Holmes's ghost to appear. And, similarly, it opened a way (a "vortex" as the elders used to say) to some evil beings from the other side, monsters created by man's imagination.'

'So, Dr Kirkby,' said Lady Conan Doyle a little nervously, 'you confirm Mr Singleton's view? A cohort of spirits is the cause of these crimes in our city?'

'Undeniably, my dear lady! On the other side, the ghosts of Victorian heroes form a compact and homogeneous group. All it needed was for one of them (and what's more, the one which had been given formidable power, energised through more than forty years of creative energy provided by Sir Arthur, vitalised with psychic energy by the imagination of thousands of readers across the planet), as I say, all it needed was for this being to find a door to access our world for the host of creatures tied to him, either closely or distantly, to invade our streets, possibly without his knowledge, and amuse themselves massacring our citizens.'

'Would my husband have been aware of the existence of his character in another world?' asked Lady Conan Doyle emotionally.

'To tell you the truth, I think he was! Your husband killed off Sherlock Holmes in a story called "The Final Problem". My friends and I thought then that this was the best solution. Holmes had achieved such popularity among the general public that we supposed that he had extraordinary vigour. At that time we were still not entirely sure that the materialisation of an imaginary hero was possible but, undoubtedly, great caution was required. A few years later, when we learnt that Conan Doyle was tempted to bring his character back to life, we judged it to be extremely dangerous. If he went through with it, the being would continue to be energised even further and, beyond a certain point of no return (the consequences of which we could not know), nothing could be done. In 1898 my brotherhood therefore decided to put your husband on his guard as to the risks involved in resurrecting his hero.'

'How did he react when you spoke to him about it?' I asked.

'When I gave him my advice, I saw that he seemed fairly shaken by what I was saying. Was he just coming to the realisation that it was not inconceivable – a realisation made all the more acute by his recent interest in spiritualist theories, which had opened his eyes to this kind of subject? Or, on the contrary, had something already convinced him that such a thing was possible?'

'Are you suggesting that the spirit of Sherlock Holmes had already manifested itself at that time?'

'As I told you, generally speaking, beings of this kind do not have the power to materialise on their own initiative. They are happy to lead their errant existence in the psychic world away from the living. But Sherlock Holmes is a unique case and has colossal energy which cannot be compared to that of the creatures I have confronted!'

'Which seems to indicate that the voice heard by Lady Conan Doyle on the night of her husband's death could have been Holmes's ghost!' cut in James, his hand on his mummified head.

'Everything points to that being so, indeed. Similarly, the meaning of the note written at the time of his death suggests that he had managed to dismiss the being and send it back to its world for a time, an effort which no doubt cost him a great deal, I fear.'

'But that's dreadful!' cried Lady Conan Doyle, bursting into tears. 'So, that night it was trying to ward off the creature he had created with such enthusiasm that exhausted him! And no one could do anything to save him!'

'I understand your pain,' I said, putting my hand on her wrist. 'But it was impossible for you and your family to do more than you had already done. You said as much yourself. He was already physically very tired . . .'

'One more thing,' intervened Dr Dryden, clinging to his scepticism. 'You talk about characters from novels and literary creations. But, as far as I know, Jack the Ripper actually existed. He was not a hero from a Victorian novel!'

'My dear doctor,' explained Ashley Kirkby, 'in this affair it is not the real murderer who interests us but the development of his character in the imagination of his time and in ours. So much has been said about the identity of Jack the Ripper (which remains one of criminal history's greatest unsolved enigmas, needless to say) that the character has become a true hero of literature, like Hyde, Dracula and co. That is why our young friends, Singleton and Trelawney, were unable to see his features. He doesn't have any! He has no definite identity – and therefore no face!'

'There is no time to lose!' James cried at the mention of the killer into whose hands we had so nearly fallen. 'We must find out how to stop these psychic monstrosities, as quickly as possible!'

'I agree,' declared Lady Conan Doyle, drying her tears. 'But what do you think you can do to stop them?'

'We will follow your husband's example,' I replied. 'All those spirits have to go back into their boxes.'

'Easier said than done!' objected Dr Dryden.

'If Sir Arthur managed it, so can we!' exclaimed James, with as much conviction as he could muster.

'I think we need to have another word with Mr Holmes,' I suggested. 'London is an immense city. Without his help, it will be like looking for a needle in a haystack. He's the one who put us on the right track for Jack the Ripper by recommending that we go to Narrow Street. We must persuade him to help us find the others.'

'And then?' fretted Dr Dryden, for whom the idea of finding himself face to face with one of these creatures was distinctly unwelcome.

'Mr Singleton has already told you: we will put them back in their boxes,' replied the little man.

'Hmm . . .'

'Dr Dryden,' I replied, 'we must go to your uncle's house straight away.'

'That is not a problem. The major left yesterday to join his wife in Devon, on the edge of the moors. The house is empty and I have the key.'

'Right, there is no time to lose!' announced James, leading by example and leaping out of his chair like a champagne cork, ready to throw himself into the attack.

'We . . . we need a medium. Just let me make a phone call. I can convince Mrs Lang . . .'

'There is no need, Dryden!' Ashley Kirkby cut in. 'I'm sure we can do without it. The spirit of Sherlock Holmes has already proved he needs no one's help to manifest himself.'

'Lady Conan Doyle, perhaps you should wait for us here?' I suggested, turning to her while Dr Dryden picked up the telephone, refusing to give in.

'That is out of the question. You never know, I am still hopeful of communicating with my husband's spirit.'

A few minutes later, ensconced as comfortably as possible in Dr Kirkby's white Ford Model T, all five of us were heading in the direction of Marylebone.

XIII

RETURN TO BAKER STREET

WHEN we arrived, Lady Conan Doyle, James and Ashley
Kirkby made for the sitting room on the ground floor
while Dr Dryden and I went up to the first floor to prepare the
room. The furniture had been put back in position after the
meeting on Friday evening and we had to push the large table,
the sofa and the armchair towards the back wall, put the chairs
in a circle in the middle of the small room and shut the thick
curtains to prevent light coming in.

This time we would have to do without the spirit cabinet.
The one used during the previous séance had been returned to
the SPR's premises. However, as Dr Kirkby had said, Sherlock
Holmes's ghost did not appear to need that kind of assistance.
If he decided not to materialise, a vocal communication
through a controller would probably be enough to persuade
him.

Once everything was ready we joined the others. Dr Dryden
was delighted to see that Dr Kirkby and James had already
helped themselves to a glass of his uncle's famous gin.

'What a marvellous idea!' he exclaimed, taking a seat next to
them at the large table. 'I think I'll join you. I need a little
refreshment.'

'The sitting room on the first floor is ready,' I announced, accepting a glass from the doctor. 'Now we are just waiting for Mr Lang.'

'They live in New Cavendish Street. They should be here soon . . .'

He did not know how right he was. No sooner had he spoken than we heard a knock at the door. Dr Dryden disappeared and came back a few moments later with young Horace and his mother, both dressed all in black. As was to be expected, Mrs Lang was slightly irritated at having to abandon the Sunday tranquillity of her home. However, she greeted the assembly politely and, recognising James and me, acknowledged our presence.

'Dr Dryden implored us to come as quickly as possible. Apparently, the situation is very serious; he spoke of the safety of thousands of people being at stake. I hope we have not been deceived, gentlemen!'

'Not at all, Mrs Lang,' I replied. 'The situation is indeed very worrying and the presence of your son is our best guarantee of success—'

An unexpected event saved us from further justification. A strange racket had broken out just above our heads; we could hear chairs flying, objects being vigorously thrown on the floor or against the walls, breaking glass and china.

'Oh dear! The ghost of Sherlock Holmes does not seem very pleased to see us,' remarked Dr Dryden.

'Listen! It has already finished,' observed Ashley Kirkby.

'Let's go up and see!' exclaimed James, as always galvanised by a whiff of mystery and danger. 'Andrew and I will go first. The rest of you, wait on the landing.'

'You didn't warn us that it would be like this!' cried Mrs Lang, alarmed for the safety of her son, which was a constant worry to her.

'If you stay behind us and do as you are told, there is no risk, I assure you,' my associate retorted.

James went up the stairs at the head of the group, followed by Dr Kirkby, Dr Dryden and myself. Behind us, Lady Conan Doyle escorted Mrs Lang and her son.

On the first-floor landing we listened carefully but all was silent on the other side of the door.

James knocked three times.

Still nothing.

Finally, he called out in a deafening voice, 'Holmes! Can you hear me? We have come to talk to you. As friends. Will you let us in?'

Still nothing.

'OK, let's go!'

He turned the handle and opened the door.

The light from the landing gave enough illumination inside the room to see that everything had been turned upside down. Chairs were on their sides, the armchair lay with its four legs up in the air near the wall, the shelves of the sideboard were empty and debris was strewn across the floor.

But there was no sign of the ghost.

James opened the door wide to let in more light. Then he entered the sitting room, checked every corner and the bedroom where we had developed that memorable photo, and then righted the armchair and other chairs (fortunately, only one was broken) and pushed aside the worst of the shattered objects with his foot.

'That's better!' he said, inviting us to come in. 'Andrew, Dr Dryden! I won't congratulate you on your tidying up.'

We entered the room and for a few moments stood in silence. Finally, having ensured that calm had definitely returned, Dr Dryden proposed that, as far as possible, we should sit in the same places as for the Friday séance: Horace on the extreme left, then Mrs Lang, James, Dr Kirkby, Lady Conan Doyle, myself and, on the extreme right, Dr Dryden.

It was about one o'clock. Outside, the day was bright and light filtered through the drawn curtains. More so than on Friday evening, we could see what was going on around us quite clearly.

'Mr Holmes!' began Dr Dryden. 'Mr Holmes! We know you're here. Show yourself please!'

A long silence followed and no one appeared.

'I think, my dear colleague, that you were right to bring your medium,' observed Dr Kirkby on my left.

Even without looking at him, I knew that Dr Dryden's face was triumphant following the compliment.

'Right . . . Horace,' he began. 'Prepare yourself. You must make contact with Mr Holmes. A spirit guide could tell us where he is. And what he is doing.'

Horace was certainly a very disciplined young man. Barely a few minutes after the doctor's request, we saw that he was shaking on his chair, his limbs prey to energetic and searing convulsions. Then his head fell against his shoulder and his entire body relaxed. Horace's spirit had plunged into the great astral ocean.

'Dr Kirkby,' asked Lady Conan Doyle, 'what will we do if

he is as violent towards us as he has been to those poor plates?'

'He was only trying to intimidate us. I don't think he will touch us. After all, it's the ghost of Sherlock Holmes, not Jack the Ripper or Mr Hyde. He is not a killer or even a scoundrel! Fortunately for us, your husband made his hero fundamentally attached to seeking truth and justice. And, let us remember, the being hiding somewhere in this sitting room is only the physical manifestation of a fictional character.'

'Thank goodness for Arthur Conan Doyle then!' proclaimed Dr Dryden.

'It has been a long time since I heard you say anything positive about my poor husband.'

'Quiet! I think I can hear something,' murmured James. 'As if something were moving very close to me. Can't you hear it?'

'It's Blanche,' said Dr Dryden, delighted. 'I would recognise her anywhere.'

At Blanche's name, I could no longer contain a shiver. I had not forgotten what the spirit had told me the first time I had participated in a séance in this room. Each word still resonated deliciously in my ears.

'In the absence of a spirit cabinet,' resumed the doctor, 'she cannot materialise. Let's wait. She will probably use Horace's body to communicate.'

We all held our breath. I felt a wave of cold air next to me, moving and caressing my left cheek and then my right. Suddenly, Horace seemed to wake from his sleep as Dr Dryden had foreseen. He sat upright on the chair, his head slightly raised, and, although he kept his eyes closed, he appeared conscious of what was happening around him. Except that it wasn't Horace sitting next to us any more.

'Good afternoon, Blanche,' began Dr Dryden. 'It is nice to see you again.'

'Good afternoon, Doctor! I am always delighted to be among you,' said a gentle female voice through the mouth of Horace. 'Oh, good afternoon, Mr Singleton! How nice to see you again too. You seem more at peace than the last time we met. The message I gave you pleased you then?'

She was speaking to me! At the séance on Friday evening my stupefaction had been such that I had remained silent. This time politeness obliged me to reply.

I tried to imagine Blanche in Horace's place, as gracious and fragile as she seemed to me from her voice.

'Good afternoon, Blanche. In truth, I was extremely moved. It was a message from my mother. I never knew her. It was the first time . . .'

'In that case you must come back and see me, Mr Singleton. I will give you more news. And, if the doctor could install a spirit cabinet, she might even materialise. I will assist her, I assure you. But I believe that today you are here for another reason. You are here for Major Hipwood's lodger – is that right?'

'Is he here, Blanche? Can you see him?' asked Dr Dryden.

'He is sitting over there, on the sofa. He is watching you. He seems very preoccupied.'

We turned as one to the sofa but for each of us it was completely empty.

'Can we talk to him?' I asked.

'I don't know if he will reply but you can try. He is listening.'

'Why will he not materialise?'

'I don't know. He has the power to do so in any case. He is giving off intense psychic energy.'

'Mr Holmes,' I began, 'this is serious. A group of despicable spirits, who are straight out of the Victorian imagination like you, are creating panic in London: Jack the Ripper, Mr Hyde, Dorian Gray, Count Dracula. For months, they have been using this city as a macabre playground. We must find them and force them to return to their world. We need your help.'

We waited but Holmes had clearly decided not to speak.

'Blanche, can you tell us what he is doing?' asked Dr Dryden.

'He has risen and is pacing up and down the sitting room. He looks like he is thinking.'

'A poor woman almost died last night!' James cut in vehemently. 'In Narrow Street, as you predicted. The victim was saved just in time but have no doubt, other tragedies will occur. We absolutely must find these creatures and prevent them committing new crimes.'

A long silence followed his words.

'Blanche, is the spirit still there?' asked Dr Dryden.

'Yes. He has just sat down again and is rubbing his chin vigorously. I cannot advise you too strongly to be careful. Ah! Now he is up again and has starting walking around once more.'

'Mr Holmes,' began Lady Conan Doyle in a surprisingly calm voice, 'I am Sir Arthur's widow. It was you, was it not, that I heard in my husband's room the night before he died?'

'Be careful!' said Blanche. 'He has stopped dead at your words and now he is standing just in front of you . . .'

'Mr Holmes,' continued Lady Conan Doyle, 'I beseech you, tell me what really happened that evening.'

All our attention was now concentrated on the space of darkness in the middle of our circle, in front of Lady Conan Doyle. Holmes was there, just in front of us.

'Mr Holmes! Mr Holmes!' she repeated.

At that moment a vaporous whitish patch appeared on the floor. It grew and grew, expanding outwards and especially upwards, like a piece of muslin moved by a powerful breeze. The luminous form grew until it reached its final size, swaying from side to side, pulsating under some powerful invisible, elusive force, and taking shape and filling out. After about thirty seconds the outline of Sherlock Holmes appeared clearly before us, transparent and phosphorescent, surrounded by a slight halo. Unlike on Friday evening, he was wearing cotton trousers with narrow stripes, a black waistcoat over his tie and a three-quarter-length jacket with a wide collar. His face seemed thinner and, above all, more concerned.

The luminescent body had turned towards Sir Arthur's widow. Holmes gazed at her intently for a long time and suddenly gave a deep bow.

'Madam,' he said, bowing, 'it is a great honour to meet you. I would have preferred it to be under different circumstances but destiny decided otherwise!'

'Oh!' Lady Conan Doyle cried, putting her hands to her cheeks. 'I would never have believed such a thing was possible! It is true then? You are the spirit of the hero created by my husband?'

'You can look at it that way, certainly. But you know, I cut the umbilical cord with my creator a long time ago and acquired my own life. In fact, from the day he decided to kill off his character, I, the ghost of Sherlock Holmes, was truly born!'

'Fascinating!' exclaimed Ashley Kirkby. 'I was always convinced that it was possible but I had never seen the . . . uh . . . living proof before!'

The spirit left our circle and went to stand between the two windows, forcing some of us to turn around to see him.

'Mr Holmes, was it you in my husband's bedroom the night he died?'

'Yes, it was. I had come to try one last time to persuade him to publish a new story.'

'Why, since you say yourself that you had acquired an independent existence a long time ago?' I asked. 'It didn't matter to you whether Conan Doyle stopped or carried on writing his stories.'

Holmes took something out of his jacket pocket and I couldn't initially see what it was because of the luminescence that blended with the vaporous halo of his body. However, I guessed that it was a pipe when he put the object between his lips and moved his hands as if to light the tobacco. Could ghosts smoke then? Yet, no smoke came out of his mouth. I suspected that he had adopted the posture simply to correspond to the image we had of him.

'You are quite mistaken,' he replied. 'Yes, I acquired a free existence in my world but that existence is not eternal. My power can decline and I will then become like those thousands of fluidic bodies wandering around in space, deprived of vitality and conscience, waiting for the final destruction. Dreadful! So, I was always very eager for Sir Arthur to continue his stories, at any cost. His need for money was often very pressing so it had never posed much of a problem until then. But in his last few years . . . well . . . I could no longer persuade him to go back on his decision to stop. He didn't even want me to write myself—'

'What?' cried James, almost indignantly. 'Do you mean that you wrote some of his stories?'

'Oh, not many, only four![12] But I say again, he did not even want to talk about that. He was exhausted, ill, weak. I knew that the end was near. And I think he was unjustly annoyed with me. He never appreciated the aspect of his work I represented. For him, all that mattered was his historical novels. One might say that the idea that future generations would only remember his detective stories after he died was intolerable to him. That evening, he was very rude to me; he insulted me, treating me as if I were a lout, and assured me that the world would be rid of me when he died, that I would not survive him, that I would deflate like an old balloon, disappearing from this world for good and from any other world at the same time. It was very painful for me. At any rate, through foolish entreaties and commands to the Almighty he managed to destroy my means to act in the real world and forced me to return to the realm of shadows. As if I were somehow to blame for the long painful slog his life had become! But when I left him he was still alive. Please, you must believe me, Lady Conan Doyle!'

'Perhaps, but this nocturnal argument did nothing to improve his health,' Dr Kirkby intervened. 'His heart gave out in the early morning.'

'That does not make me a murderer! I would never be capable of such ignominy!'

With these last words, he threw back his shoulders and pointed his pipe at us. It was almost comical. It was difficult to know whether he was acting or if he was entirely sincere. How can you know what a spirit feels?

'Mr Holmes, why then did you come back to this world and haunt my uncle's house?' demanded Dr Dryden.

'I have already told you. It is most important for me that Sir Arthur's work is celebrated for as long as possible. It is the best guarantee of my psychic power. Today, you see me on good form and I intend to stay that way! What better publicity could there be for my creator's stories than the presence of the ghost of Sherlock Holmes himself at 221 Baker Street, while thousands of people from across the world continue to write to me and show me their love? You know, Doctor, one of my greatest pleasures is to come down in the night to the ground-floor sitting room to read and reread all those letters in your uncle's sideboard. As soon as it is known that a spirit is living here, the number of letters will increase and increase . . .'

'Your obsession with your own survival is tarnishing Sherlock Holmes's reputation for greatness and nobility!' retorted Lady Conan Doyle.

'Really, Holmes! You have led in your wake the worst mob ever seen! Are you even aware of that, damn it?' cried James provocatively.

Sherlock Holmes rewarded my companion with a look as searing as the midday sun. I feared that he would decide to make the rest of the crockery fly around the room. But the spirit controlled his anger and replied, almost calmly, 'I accept all your criticisms, absolutely all of them. Moreover, I willingly concede that my "obsession with my own survival", as you put it so elegantly, Lady Conan Doyle, has long blinded me to the atrocities committed a few yards from here by those creatures of the night. My spirit was too busy looking after itself. It was an unforgivable weakness. But must I remind you that you have the greatest human bloodhound of all time standing before you? The king of detectives? The best investigator the civilised world has ever known? And you can be sure of one thing: as soon as I understood what was being plotted, I immediately tried to thwart the pernicious activity of that group of scoundrels.'

'Were you already doing battle with them when you appeared at the first séance?'

'Truthfully, at that time I was only on the trail of Jack the Ripper. During that meeting, I was told that a Member of Parliament had just been murdered in the Strand and, by chance, you informed me of another series of crimes in Chicksand Street and Jamaica Lane. I realised the full extent of the tragedy at that moment: there were many more of them than I had first believed.'

'Very well! But how did you know that Jack the Ripper was going to commit another murder in Narrow Street?' asked James, elated to find that Sherlock Holmes faithfully corresponded to the image he had venerated since childhood: a brave and honest hero, passionate about justice and integrity.

'Thanks to a telepathic link I had managed to establish without his knowledge and which had allowed me to prevent his crimes on several occasions. But he must have suspected the existence of the connection because it has become impossible to precisely anticipate his movements and acts. On

Friday night I received several contradictory messages: one located the scene of his crime near Stepney Green, another at Oxford Street, and yet another at Narrow Street. Now, even as an ethereal spirit I cannot be in several places at once! Stepney Green and Oxford Street are fairly close to one another so I could easily navigate between them. But Narrow Street was too far away. I was unwise enough to believe that you could give me your assistance and I nearly had your deaths on my conscience! I do not want to put anyone's life in danger. So, I ask you now: stay out of this! It will only lead to more death . . .'

'Thanks to Dr Kirkby,' I countered, 'we managed to stop Jack the Ripper committing his crime. The doctor has some experience of creatures from the other side and his knowledge will be valuable in the battle we are going to wage against them. Be in no doubt, Mr Holmes: with or without you, we will rid the city of these villains.'

'Well said, Andrew!' said James, raising his fist.

'The situation is serious. We must all work together,' added Ashley Kirkby.

Dr Dryden was about to speak but Lady Conan Doyle beat him to it.

'We must not hesitate for a moment!' she cried resolutely.

Turning to me, she added, 'I'm going to come with you, gentlemen, and I won't be put off.'

Dr Dryden closed his mouth without saying what he had been about to say.

'Well! It's your choice!' Sherlock Holmes flopped into his armchair. He seemed deep in a whirl of sombre and contradictory thoughts, his pipe in his mouth, his arms hanging loosely, his long legs spread out before him.

'Ah, if only Watson were with me!' we heard him mutter.

'Yes indeed!' murmured Dr Dryden in surprise. 'Where has the good doctor gone? In Conan Doyle's stories they were inseparable, those two!'

'Time is short,' I said, cutting off speculation about Watson. 'We must come up with a strategy as quickly as possible. Tonight more innocent people might be killed. Perhaps we can at least anticipate where they will attack!'

'The psychic link with the spirit of Jack the Ripper is damaged,' Holmes reminded us sadly, lifting his head so that his emaciated face could be seen above his shoulders. 'As for the others, I have never intercepted anything that could tell me about their plans.'

Dr Kirkby slowly repositioned his yellow cap on his head and then declared, 'According to Mr Singleton's earlier explanation about the resemblance of the murders over the last few weeks to those described in famous novels, it would seem that these monsters are still, in some respects, prisoners of the books in which they are the heroes. In other words, for the moment at least they are all reliving the same scenario, haunting the same places, those where they committed their imaginary crimes.'

'Why do you say "for the moment"?'

'Because I very much fear that each new crime is increasing their psychic energy and, therefore, releasing them from such pre-established scenarios. They must be neutralised before one of them is totally released. After that, he will become uncontrollable.'

'Andrew, now is the time to use your literary knowledge!' James cried. 'Which of these fiends is the most evil: Hyde? Gray? Jack the Ripper? Or the Count with the fearsome teeth?'

'Let's see . . .' I said, racking my brains. 'In Oscar Wilde's novel, Dorian Gray was only charged with one actual murder, that of the painter Basil Hallward. The other deaths with which his conscience reproached him were either suicides or accidents. Gray is immoral, cowardly, odious, whatever you like, but he is not really a habitual killer.

'The character of Mr Hyde also only committed a single murder, that of Sir Danvers Carew. However, Dr Jekyll had bought and furnished a house in Soho and Stevenson briefly lets it be understood in the final chapter that Hyde had committed loathsome deeds of great depravity, torturing his victims, probably prostitutes, with bestial desire.

'Five crimes are officially attributed to Jack the Ripper: Mary Ann Nichols, Annie Chapman, Elizabeth Stride, Catherine Eddowes and Mary Kelly. But other "uncertified" victims are sometimes also attributed to him: Emma Elizabeth Smith, Martha Tabram, Alice McKenzie, possibly Frances Coles as well . . .

'As for Count Dracula's victims, that calculation is much more difficult. Let's see . . . There is of course Lucy Westenra who was bitten by the vampire during one of the young lady's frequent sleepwalking episodes. There is Renfield, the patient treated by Dr Seward in his lunatic asylum, who was careless enough to put Mina Harker on her guard against the Count. Then there is the crew of the *Demeter*, the ship which was travelling to England with the box containing Dracula's body on board. During the voyage, the sailors are victims of a mysterious curse which kills them one after the other. Bram Stoker presented the Count as the incarnation of Evil, and his supernatural gifts and the fact that he lived for centuries gives him the most terrifying record of all. Yes, if we have to choose one, it is undoubtedly Dracula who is the most dangerous of all!'

'Wonderful!' said Holmes, suddenly getting up from his armchair. 'Watson used to commend my knowledge of sensational literature. But, well, I bow to your superior expertise! I am impressed by so much culture. Now, young man, can you tell us the places favoured by Count Dracula?'

'If I remember rightly, the Count sent fifty boxes containing Transylvanian earth from his castle in the Carpathians to England, to a property he had bought in the London suburbs, in Carfax near Purfleet. However, to cover his back, he did not keep all the boxes at the same address. He had some delivered to three other places he owned: a house in Chicksand Street, another in Jamaica Lane in Bermondsey and a large house in Piccadilly. To complete the vampire's crimes, let me remind you that Lucy Westenra was bitten in Whitby, where the *Demeter* sank . . .'

'Whitby? Where's that?' asked James.

'In Yorkshire,' replied Dr Dryden. 'More than two hundred miles from here.'

'The papers have not said anything in particular about Whitby,' I said. 'Or about Purfleet, I believe. However, they did mention Chicksand Street and Bermondsey.'

'Piccadilly runs along the northern side of Green Park,'

added Dr Kirkby. 'Victims were found in Green Park too. Evidently, Dracula's murderous work is concentrated in these three places. I think that is where we should focus our efforts.'

'That's all well and good, but what can we do to stop him if we find ourselves face to face with him?'

'We will use this!' The little man lifted the side of his jacket and withdrew his bowie knife. This frightened Sherlock Holmes's ghost so much that he leapt up and sought refuge behind the sofa without saying a word, pretending to think while he chewed on his pipe.

'Phantoms are afraid of swords and any sharp object which might puncture their energy. All it needs is one thrust and they are rendered harmless,' explained Dr Kirkby.

'Nonsense!' cried Dr Dryden. 'Those are just guesses arrived at during your home-made experiments!'

'I assure you that it is not a guess. It has been confirmed by several occultist witnesses who have had brushes with leading spirits. And let me remind you, my dear colleague, that this is how I made the ghost of Jack the Ripper flee. My intervention on behalf of our friends here is proof that it works!'

'And Mr Holmes's concern appears to prove you right, also,' said Lady Conan Doyle, amused to observe the psychic being who was still taking cover behind the padded back of the sofa.

'At least let us warn Scotland Yard,' pressed Dr Dryden.

'Wonderful! I can imagine the expression on the inspectors' faces when you explain the situation!' exclaimed Kirkby. 'No, we must all arm ourselves as quickly as possible with knives!'

'That will not be a problem,' Dr Dryden said proudly, not

wanting to look like a coward in front of Lady Conan Doyle. 'My uncle's office contains a collection of knives and stilettos from the East Indies the likes of which you have never seen!'

XIV

A FEW HOURS' WELL-DESERVED REST

THE night before had been long and turbulent for some of us and we needed a good rest before another wakeful night. After taking leave of Blanche and Sherlock Holmes, the séance came to an end and the group separated, having decided on a strategy for our ghost hunt.

The word strategy might be an exaggeration because in the end we did not really have much choice. Once the temptation to turn to outside assistance had been rejected (how could others be asked to believe our story in a few minutes when we ourselves had needed several days?), our mission was nothing less than to watch three streets located in three different areas of the capital. It had been agreed that Drs Kirkby and Dryden would watch Chicksand Street, Lady Conan Doyle and James (my gallant friend having immediately suggested that he work with the only woman in the group) would be responsible for Jamaica Lane, and Holmes and I would go to Piccadilly. Each team would begin their vigil at eleven o'clock and we would all meet at 221 Baker Street at five o'clock the following morning.

This plan of attack had one major problem: it left the rest of the city free for one of the other murderous phantoms. But the most important thing was to prevent Dracula from developing his own personality and will, as Sherlock Holmes had done.[13]

As destiny had designated his colleague to be his team mate, Dr Dryden had obligingly suggested that Dr Kirkby keep him company at Major Hipwood's house until the evening. Goodness only knows what they would talk about during those long hours! There was not enough time for Lady Conan Doyle to return to Windlesham beforehand so she had preferred to go to Sir Arthur's London apartment near Victoria Station where James would meet her at about ten thirty. As for Horace and his Cerberus of a mother, it was out of the question to involve them further in this affair without risking serious repercussions. They had returned home to New Cavendish Street as soon as the séance had finished.

Before parting, Dr Dryden led us into his uncle's office where he solemnly gave each of us a weapon from among the fifty specimens attached to the walls. Lady Conan Doyle received a splendid Indian dagger, as light and easy to handle as it is possible for that kind of instrument to be; Dr Dryden opted for a Kanjar with a handle in the shape of a pistol; my friend came out armed with an impressive Tamil Pichangatti knife; as for myself, I was now wearing a kukri dagger, used, according to the doctor, by Gurkha warrior chiefs. I had awkwardly attached its heavy silver sheath to my trouser belt and it grazed my thigh throughout the return journey by car.

We reached our rooms in Montague Street just after five o'clock. As a veritable man of action James knew that he had to take care of his mind and body to perform at his best. He immediately went to lie down in his room, recommending that I do the same. However, unlike my friend, the prospect of danger was making me quite nervous. I swapped my kukri dagger for Bram Stoker's novel, which was lying on my desk, then, ensconced on the sofa in the sitting room, my cigarette holder between my lips, I began to leaf through the book.

To reassure myself that I had not missed any of the places where the vampire had committed his crimes, I drew up a list on a piece of paper, happy that this time I was able to verify them. Having eliminated far-off places like Whitby and Purfleet since their provincial calm had remained undisturbed over the last few months (I checked in the available newspapers), I was left, as before, with the names of Jamaica Lane, Chicksand Street and Piccadilly. What is more, apart from Jamaica Lane where the author was rather vague, I noticed that Stoker was extremely precise about the addresses: at Chicksand Street the Count was supposed to have had his boxes delivered to No. 197; the large house in Piccadilly was located at No. 347 exactly. Better still, he had given a proper description. It was a large, tall stone building, distinguishable from all the others by a flight of steps and a bow window, two or three houses along from a large white church near the Junior Constitutional. Assuming Stoker had taken inspiration from a real house in Piccadilly, even if the numbers had been invented, it was highly likely that the psychic being had set up home there. That night I would be responsible for keeping watch on that house! Fortunately, Sherlock Holmes would be there . . . and, presumably, one should be less afraid of confronting ghosts when one has a ghost on one's side . . .

What is more, my reading revealed the incredible topicality of some passages from the novel. It made my blood run cold. In Chapter XVIII it was as if the author were addressing his words to us: 'The nosferatu do not die like the bee when he sting once.

He is only stronger, and being stronger, have yet more power to work evil.' And what should be made of this strange conversation between Mina and Professor Van Helsing in Chapter XXV? 'The criminal always work at one crime, that is the true criminal who seems predestinate to crime, and who will of none other . . . He is clever and cunning and resourceful . . . In a difficulty he has to seek resource in habit. His past is a clue . . .' Was this not confirmation of Dr Kirkby's theory, according to which Dracula and the other spirits were compelled to reproduce the crimes of the novels in which they had been created?

Gradually I drifted off into a sleep filled with unpleasant dreams. In the last (the only one I still remember) a breathtaking fall plunged me into the depths of an endless abyss as a group of creatures spiralled around me, making unbearable shrieking noises. With each turn these devils tightened the circle in their macabre dance, their fluidic bodies lighting the chasm into which I was ineluctably sinking, unable to resist the fatal force. As their fluid, slimy, disgusting faces swirled around me, gurgling just a few inches from my own, I saw stilettos reflected in their sinister eyes, each with a more elaborate and extravagant blade than the one before and whose sharp points were just waiting to cut my stomach to pieces.

Shaking me violently by the shoulder, James saved me from that imaginary hell and prevented the first blow of the knife.

'Hey!' he said, placing my book, which had fallen on the floor, on top of my head. 'Reading doesn't seem to be very good for you. You're as white as a sheet.'

James was freshly shaved, wearing black trousers and a

stylish black jacket with a round collar. He was playing with Major Hipwood's Indian knife. My associate radiated good health; he was ready to fight any battles against crime – whether against the living or the dead. He didn't seem to care!

'What time is it?' I asked, sitting up on the sofa, my face creased with sleep.

'Gone half past eight. Come on, my friend! You need to keep your strength up, I'm taking you to Meredith's. And I'm dying of hunger too! Who knows? Maybe it will be our last meal!'

He told jokes too.

Although my stomach was in knots, it appeared wiser to eat first.

As I had no intention of competing in the fashion stakes, I was ready quickly, choosing an informal outfit of velvet trousers and jacket together with a thick cap. Then, as our friends Dryden and Kirkby were going to Mile End Town that evening, I asked the telephone operator for Major Hipwood's number. When I had his nephew at the end of the line I told him what I had discovered and strongly advised him to watch the area around 197 Chicksand Street.

Hanging up, I slipped the kukri knife into the left-hand pocket of my overcoat and Bram Stoker's novel into the right, and followed James out of the house. It was unseasonably cold for the start of summer. We walked up the street to Russell Square and sat at a table in the large restaurant. I only managed to eat a frugal meal but James had a hearty appetite, as well as a disarming lack of concern. Despite all my efforts to encourage him to take extreme care, my friend constantly returned to the reason for his unfailing cheerfulness: the tremendous possibilities for adventure and mystery which he supposed had opened up for us now. The same phrase returned to his lips like a leitmotiv between mouthfuls of jellied game or meat pie.

'My word! Imagine, in our first case we meet the ghosts of Sherlock Holmes, Jack the Ripper and Dracula! It's more than we could ever have hoped for, Andrew! No one will believe it!'

And before each mouthful of vintage white wine, he clinked his glass against mine, which I had long since abandoned on the table.

At quarter past ten James asked for the bill and we left the restaurant to walk silently to the junction with Great Russell Street.

Standing beside the few vehicles that were parked on the street, my friend shook my hand for a long time and only then did I see for a second a shadow of anxiety in his eyes. But he did not leave us time to dwell upon it. Before I could say a word, he leapt into a cab which revved its engine and I watched it disappear into the distance at the corner of Bloomsbury Street.

It had started to drizzle. I got into the next taxi.

'Piccadilly please. Number 347!'

XV

THE SEARCH FOR THE PICCADILLY HOUSE

AFTER passing Piccadilly Circus, the taxi slowed down and stopped at the top of the famous London artery, just after the junction with Regent Street. It was a little after quarter to eleven.

'Are you sure it's here?' I asked, slightly disappointed with my urban surroundings.

'Definitely, sir. Look, over there on your left, after the ABC Café. It's written on the plaque: Number 347!'

Intrigued, I got my book out of my coat pocket. It did not make sense. In Chapter XXII Jonathan Harker, Dr Seward and Van Helsing sat on a bench in Green Park and observed the house. Having taken the time before leaving to study our old map of London over the mantelpiece, I knew that the park was much further down the road. I quickly skimmed the relevant passage. In his journal Jonathan Harker indicated that: 'At the corner of Arlington Street our contingent got out and strolled into the Green Park. My heart beat as I saw the house on which so much of our hope was centred, looming up grim and silent in its deserted condition amongst its more lively and spruce-looking neighbours.'

'Keep going please and drop me at the corner of Arlington Street.'

'As you wish, sir!'

The taxi moved forward again for about three hundred yards before stopping again.

'This is Arlington Street.'

'But I can't see the park anywhere! Where is Green Park?'

'In front of us. We have to go a bit further on.'

'Fine, drop me at the start of the park then.'

'Yes, sir.'

The taxi travelled one hundred yards at a slow speed. This time I had reached my destination. In front of me, on my left, were the railings of Green Park. On the other side of the road was a long row of houses, each more affluent than the one before.

'What are you looking for exactly, sir?'

'A house . . . which faces the park.'

'If you don't have the number, you won't find it easy,' said the driver, whistling through his teeth. 'Green Park is enormous. The railings follow Piccadilly for five hundred yards. The best thing would be to drive to Hyde Park Corner. Maybe you'll recognise what you're looking for on the way!'

'No, no! Let me out here,' I said, shivering at the very idea of walking the streets for hours under a curtain of drizzle.

Anyway, I had an appointment with Sherlock Holmes, did I not?

I got out of the cab, paid the driver and lit a cigarette.

Traffic was almost nonexistent at this hour, apart from a few taxis, which were empty. Similarly, the pavements were practically deserted. One would need a very good reason to be out in such weather.

I followed the railings of Green Park, unconsciously keeping close to the kerb in order to stay under the light of the streetlamps. Of course, I knew that this was the West End. Nestling between Mayfair, Soho and Westminster, Piccadilly was one of the richest areas in the capital. It was nothing like the sordid, sombre streets of Whitechapel. And yet . . . Just to my left the park was closed for the night and formed a dark, freezing, threatening expanse. I was unable to stop myself imagining that strange creatures were watching me just behind the railings, which offered no protection whatsoever.

After twenty minutes I reached Hamilton Place. Having covered the entire length of Piccadilly that ran alongside the park, I had found nothing that exactly corresponded to Bram Stoker's description. There was no sign of the white church either.

And although it was now nearly half past eleven, Sherlock Holmes's ghost was proving to be just as elusive as the object of my search.

I decided to try a different tack. Leafing through my book again, protected from the rain by an old oak tree the branches of which had spread right over the streetlamp, I read out loud a sentence from Jonathan Harker's journal: "'Beyond the Junior Constitutional I came across the house described and was satisfied that this was the next of the lairs arranged by Dracula.'"

By mentioning the Junior Constitutional was Stoker providing a serious clue? I knew that Victorian London had had a large number of gentlemen's clubs, private societies whose elected members (MPs, scientists, academics, men of letters) enjoyed meeting in illustrious company. But how could I be sure that the Junior Constitutional had really existed?

I crossed the road and retraced my steps, this time scrutinising the bronze plaques at the entrance to each house. I found the Junior Athenaeum Club at No. 116, about a third of the way along, by Down Street. If my memories of reading Dickens were correct, its hour of glory had been at the end of the 1860s. It was a splendid large house. On the façade, near the door, a plaque indicated that it had previously been occupied by the Duke of Newcastle and built by his father-in-law, Mr Adrian Hope.

I stepped back into the road in order to see the high façades of the neighbouring buildings. One of them, to which I had not paid much attention earlier when I was inspecting them from the other side of the road, seemed worthy of closer scrutiny: an opulent old house standing four storeys high and with a bow window and a flight of steps up to the door. Here, there was no sign of dust covering the windows or shutters, and no dirty panelling blackened over time; nor was there any paint flaking off the ornamental ironwork. But the house was giving off an unmistakable whiff of strangeness that could not fail to attract the interest of readers of *Dracula*. The problem was of course that the Junior Athenaeum was not the Junior Constitutional. Perhaps Bram Stoker had made a mistake. Reluctantly, I decided to continue to Piccadilly Circus.

In the end, it did not take me long to find what I was looking for. A hundred and fifty yards further on, halfway between Half Moon Street and Clarges Street, on one of the pillars flanking the enormous gates to a large house, the curious passer-by could read: *Junior Constitutional Club. Founded in 1887. Strictly members only*. This time I thought I had reached my destination.

But my joy was short-lived. It was clear that nothing near the Club, including the area up to Stratton Street and White Horse Street, remotely matched the description Harker had given of the vampire's house.

So what of this mysterious club? Was the Junior Athenaeum the one I was looking for after all? It was the most likely explanation.

So I turned around again and quickly retraced my steps to the house with the bow window, a few dozen yards from the Junior Athenaeum just after Down Street. There were lights at several windows on the second floor, which suggested that the owner was currently in residence. Did he know that his home was possibly also being used as a refuge for the ghost of Count Dracula?

Despite my overcoat and my velvet cap, the rain had long soaked me to the skin. I was tired and chilled. And the night had only just begun!

Between the house and its neighbour on the right was a tiny alleyway, which probably led to the tradesman's entrance. The wind had got up but the alleyway was sheltered from the rain. I decided to take refuge there while I thought about what I should do. As always when I found myself in the heart of the action, feverish indecision swept over me. If only James had been with me! He would have known what to do! Should I knock at the door and ask the butler if he had recently come across the ghost of a vampire in his master's home? Or should I patrol the entire length of Piccadilly – alone, over a distance of five hundred yards, as the taxi driver had said – to check that no crime was being committed?

Without conviction, I chose a third option, which I found about as attractive as the other two. I decided to stay where I was next to the house, slightly inside the alley, to observe the surrounding area and wait for something, whatever it was, to happen.

For the next hour – and how long time can seem sometimes! – I saw only the occasional figure pass the house and, without exception, they all continued on their way without slowing down or showing any interest in the building in whose shadow I was heroically shivering. Understandably, they were hurrying home to the warm.

Without a doubt, keeping watch on a house where Dracula's ghost might be lying low is not like keeping watch on any other house. Although I soon sank into a sweet, soothing torpor in reaction to the cold and my own exhaustion, whenever I awoke to the reality of the situation I was overwhelmed with nervous energy which I had great difficulty containing and which almost suffocated me. I felt the invisible, pernicious fluid of the vampire floating around me, patiently waiting for the right moment to materialise and plant his sharpened canines in my throat.

It was while I was in this state of mind that an incident occurred which really tested my nerves. Behind me, at the other end of the alleyway, I suddenly had the terrifying impression that someone had just spoken my name. My hair stood on end and every muscle in my body was so tense that an entire minute went by before I managed to turn my head to the side. To my very great relief, I could see that the alleyway behind me was just as empty as it had been before.

Had I dreamt the words out of exhaustion? Or was Sherlock

Holmes nearby and calling for me? But if he was, why did he not show himself straight away instead of trying to give me a heart attack?

To reassure myself that the premises really were deserted, I gathered what was left of my courage and walked slowly and deliberately down towards the other end of the alleyway. It was thirty yards long and on one side opened onto a small courtyard, behind the house, leading to what looked like some old stables. Access to the courtyard from the alleyway was blocked by a large iron gate, locked from the inside with several heavy metal chains. The alleyway itself came to an abrupt end in a high wall.

From what I could tell, there was nothing and no one hiding in this sinister place.

I was preparing to go back when suddenly I heard my name again, this time very distinctly.

'Mr Singleton! Mr Singleton!'

I recoiled in fear. The voice (and the most frightening thing was that it was not Sherlock Holmes's voice) seemed to come from behind the gate, although I could not make out any shadows between the bars. Attempting to recover my wits, I was slowly approaching the gate and opening my mouth to speak when the voice addressed me from behind my shoulder.

'Mr Singleton! Mr Singleton!'

I turned around, shoving my coat out of the way and clumsily groping for the kukri knife. Six inches in front of me, by the wall of the neighbouring house, a vaporous column made of the same viscous, streaked substance as that which had appeared in the centre of the circle during the séances rose in the air. The column very quickly took on a firmer consistency like a shower of snow crystallising in extreme cold. As it became more concentrated, I could soon see the outline of a solidly built man of about five foot nine. The legs were powerful, the arms short, with gloved hands; the determined-looking face was adorned with a wonderful moustache and the luminescent eyes seemed to sparkle with mischief and kindliness. Soon the entity had materialised from head to foot, dressed elegantly in the fashion of the last century in a light cotton suit, a coat with a black collar and a bowler hat.

The impeccably dressed ghost advanced towards me with an engaging smile.

'Mr Singleton, do not fear!' he declared, glancing at the handle of the knife still clenched in my fingers. 'I am awfully sorry that I frightened you. Mr Holmes asked me to warn you.'

'Holme—? Holmes?' I stammered. 'How do you know Sherlock Holmes?'

'Well, we have actually known each other for a long time! My name is Watson. Dr John H. Watson.'

'Dr . . . Watson?'

Was there to be no end to the surprises that evening?

'We concluded from your absence that you had fallen out with Sherlock Holmes and you no longer wanted to see him,' I said. 'He seemed very upset about it.'

'Ha! I hope he was! Success most definitely went to his head. Thanks to his excessive thirst for immortality, he behaved towards our creator in a way that I entirely condemned and this led me to keep my distance. However, I promised myself that if he returned to normal I would come back to him. That seemed to be the case so here I am! You know, Holmes really is an exceptional person . . . when he is not being a monstrous egotist!'

'I had arranged to meet him at eleven o'clock but he hasn't come. I've been worried sick. What did he want you to tell me?'

'That we were mistaken, Mr Singleton. Initially, Holmes came to the same conclusion as you concerning this place. He too was certain that Dracula's ghost had sought refuge in this house belonging to Mr Thaddeus Jenkin. But we have searched it from top to bottom. The Count is not here now, that much is clear. This place does seem to be the one used by Bram Stoker for his vampire's den though.'

'Where is he hiding then? Does your friend have any idea?'

'Holmes was in a strange mood,' continued Dr Watson, not seeming to notice my question. 'He was pacing up and down with his pipe in his mouth, in one of those periods of reflection when it is better not to disturb him. Eventually, his face cleared suddenly and he led me off without delay.'

'Very good! But tell me quickly where Holmes went!'

'To Highgate Cemetery,' he replied, rolling the end of his ectoplasm moustache between his fingers.

'Highgate Cemetery?'

'It is a few miles from here, in north London near Hampstead Heath, just beyond Camden Town. I was there only a moment ago. Before sending me to warn you, Holmes wanted to be sure that he was not mistaken. But from what we saw, there is no doubt that something strange is going on over there. You see . . .

'Mr Singleton,' he resumed, the urgency of the situation

suddenly coming back to him, 'you must join Sherlock Holmes in Highgate as soon as possible.'

'I have to warn the others first. It is already half past one and if Holmes is right we'll need everyone.'

'Very well. You go on ahead and I will warn your companions. It will only take me a few minutes.'

Before I had even moved a muscle, Dr Watson's translucent form had disappeared into the night. The good doctor was undoubtedly right. I should not waste any time. We had at all costs to prevent those monsters committing any more crimes in order to stop them becoming stronger, more unpredictable and more uncontrollable.

'For humanity itself!' Lady Conan Doyle had predicted a few days ago. For the first time since the beginning of the adventure I was truly convinced of the great importance of our mission. And I felt suddenly and unexpectedly filled with passion and prodigious courage.

A minute later I was in the back seat of a cab and speeding north in the direction of Hampstead and London's famous necropolis.

XVI

AT HIGHGATE CEMETERY

H IGHGATE'S immense cemetery lay to the west of Hampstead Heath, a gloomy park with dead-looking grass, rushes and wild flowers as far as the eye could see. Established in 1839, the cemetery had a strange, striking charm that might have come straight out of a baroque poem. It would be more correct to refer to Highgate's *cemeteries* because, in reality, the necropolis was split into two distinct parts. In 1854, faced with the constantly rising number of burials, the London Cemetery Company had been forced to buy additional plots of land and create a second area adjoining the first on the other side of Swains Lane.

The cemetery has always been considered haunted. Since its creation, inhabitants of the surrounding area have described how, during a full moon, the dead rise from their graves and wander around the tree-lined avenues, not far from the one reserved for the excommunicated, parricides and other killers of all kinds.

In the eighteenth century it was also said that a coffin from Turkey which had been placed in a chapel at Highgate contained the body of a vampire.

However, for many, its macabre reputation was due, above all, to the tragic events surrounding the death of Elizabeth

Siddal, wife of the Pre-Raphaelite painter Dante Gabriel Rossetti.

When Lizzie killed herself in February 1862 after taking a dose of laudanum which was ten times stronger than the dose prescribed to help her overcome serious depression, Rossetti was with his mistress. Overwhelmed with pain and contrition, he buried his wife's body with great pomp at Highgate Cemetery and left the manuscript of a collection of poems he had just completed in her coffin. In autumn 1869, on the advice of a blackmailer named Charles Augustus Howell, Rossetti had the tomb reopened and removed the manuscript. To the amazement of the few witnesses present during that ghoulish ceremony, Elizabeth Siddal's hair was not only still as golden as on the day of her death, seven years before, it had also grown considerably and her body was perfectly preserved. The legend of the female vampire of Highgate was born. As for Rossetti, he in turn fell prey to severe depression, embracing the excesses of opium and alcohol.

A malicious rumour hinted that it was Bram Stoker himself who had advised Rossetti to exhume the body. Of course, this was totally unfounded. Stoker simply recalled the episode when he was creating the character of Lucy Westenra for his novel *Dracula*.

Charles Augustus Howell, the real mastermind behind the exhumation, unwittingly found literary fame. In April 1904 Arthur Conan Doyle, who knew nothing of the details of the Elizabeth Siddal affair, published a Sherlock Holmes story called 'The Adventure of Charles Augustus Milverton', set in Hampstead. The writer created a vitriolic portrait of the blackmailer.

Obviously, I knew none of this when the taxi slowed down in front of the chapel located near the entrance to the cemetery in Swains Lane. Dr Kirkby only told me of these London chronicles, and many other things besides, a few days later. For him, it was clear that, whether they were true or not, all these elements connecting Bram Stoker and Conan Doyle to a tale of the supernatural and vampirism had formed a sickening astral compound over Highgate, which the monsters had fed on with delight.

The rain had stopped as we passed Regent's Park, to be replaced by fog after Camden Town, which stayed with us on our journey.

'Is this the place, sir? Are you certain?' asked the driver, who was decidedly unsure about my choice of destination that night.

'Absolutely, my dear fellow,' I replied through the window. Turning to the red brick wall, I added, 'I have an appointment of the greatest importance.'

'Well, in that case . . .'

He leant across to close the door, turned his vehicle around with a screeching of tyres and fled towards the reassuring lights of the city.

I climbed the wall without difficulty and, once at the top, tried to work out the layout of the cemetery – or as much as the pale moonlight, particularly dense vegetation and sheets of fog, which literally seemed to come out of the earth, would allow me. Four main avenues led away from the entrance; I was perched on the wall to the left. These avenues wound their way through an immense expanse of white tombs and vaults, some intact and others half opened, and headed northwest into the depths of the cemetery where I could just make out through the darkness shapes of elaborate buildings.

After this rapid examination, I jumped down lightly from the wall. I chose the avenue opposite me, which from a height had appeared to take the most direct route through the cemetery. I advanced about fifty steps through the sepulchres. The atmosphere was sombre. It felt as though the tombstones I passed were alive and that the white crosses above them were turning to watch me as I went by.

At a crossroads, I stood quietly for a few minutes, waiting for a sign of Sherlock Holmes's presence. To my great disappointment, the silence was deafening.

Undoubtedly, it was not easy to be Holmes's assistant. He seemed to just please himself and I could only admire the good Dr Watson even further for accompanying him throughout his many adventures and putting up with his moods.

Without a clue as to where Holmes was hiding and not knowing which direction to take, I continued on my way, trusting to luck that I would find the buildings I had seen earlier at the far end of the cemetery. The avenues were so tortuous that after three-quarters of an hour I found myself at a junction I had already visited. I was going round in circles and might continue for a long time if the person I was looking for did not decide to show himself.

'Holmes, where are you, damn it! Holmes! Holmes!' I grumbled softly at the edge of a path.

Just to add to my ordeal, the fog was getting thicker, brushing the ground like a viscous blanket.

I waited for a few more minutes, wandering around the

crossroads like a lost soul. Finally, as I was preparing to head for the avenue at right angles to the one I had already taken, I recognised the famous detective's deep voice coming from far away, the words no more than a whisper.

'Singleton! I'm here. Come quickly!'

I could not see him but the call distinctly came from the path going northeast.

'It's about time!' I said, feeling rather annoyed as I hurried over.

'Quiet!' I heard him say a few inches from me.

Sherlock Holmes's willowy body had suddenly appeared at my side out of the fog that hid my own feet from view. The powerful phosphorescence as he materialised briefly lit up the macabre landscape surrounding me.

'Don't make a sound! The monsters we are tracking are two hundred yards from here.'

'Monsters? Plural?'

'Hyde, Dorian Gray, Jack the Ripper . . . and Dracula of course. None ignored the call. As I speak, they are hiding in the City of the Dead.'

'What's that?'

'A very old part of the cemetery, built along the lines of Egyptian mausoleums. It is the ideal place to carry out their lethal business.'

'But tell me something, Holmes. Hampstead is not the usual hunting ground of these scoundrels. What is the connection between them and Highgate Cemetery?'

'Simple, my dear friend. The little man with the cap . . . what is his name now? Ah, yes, Dr Kirkby! Well, Dr Kirkby foresaw the solution: until they have been freed from their pre-established scenarios, these beings remain prisoners of the novels in which they feature. Simply put, what no one had envisaged was that this emancipation had already begun! Earlier, in Piccadilly, when I realised that Dracula was not in the house where I had been sure of flushing him out, I asked myself what other location he might haunt at that time. I thought again of the various crime scenes you described from memory for us this afternoon. With regard to the novel *Dracula*, you listed five addresses: Carfax, Whitby, Chicksand Street, Jamaica Lane and Piccadilly. Immediately and very logically we eliminated the first two. But had we forgotten one?'

'I have thought about that list dozens of times since!' I said. 'But I don't think I was mistaken . . .'

'Oh, don't worry. You were looking for places in the novel where Dracula himself had revealed his presence. As I have just said, it is probably because the character is now freed from the original plot that he has the power to materialise elsewhere. For example, in a place where his presence had never been explicitly noted but which was nonetheless connected to him.'

'In that case, the field is immense. Where did you start?'

'At the beginning!' Holmes taunted, pointing his finger emphatically at the sky. 'In the list of actual crimes committed over the last few weeks, you do not seem to have paid much attention to the disappearance of children reported at Hampstead police station. The capital's largest cemetery is next to the heath! What could be more natural for a vampire than to roam among the graves?'

'If my memories of the novel are correct, Bram Stoker only

mentioned one cemetery in London – Kingstead.'

'Yes, but there is no such cemetery in our beautiful capital. For some obscure reason Bram Stoker changed the name. When he speaks of Kingstead he most assuredly meant where we are now. Come, young man, use that formidable memory of yours again. Remember what happened at the cemetery in Kingstead and everything will become clear.'

'Good heavens!' I cried, slapping my thigh. 'Why didn't I think of it earlier? Lucy Westenra kidnapped several children on Hampstead Heath. Most of them were found unconscious with a strange bite on their necks. As for Kingstead, it was none other than the place where Lucy was buried. That was also where Van Helsing, Lord Godalming, Quincey Morris and Dr Seward opened her coffin by night, stuck a stake in her heart and decapitated her to free her from the Count's influence and give her eternal peace.'

'Aha! You got there at last! So you see why, put that way, this place is strangely important to Dracula's ghost. This is where he dreams of having his revenge on the living – there is no doubt about it. But just a moment – where is my dear Dr Watson? He should have come back with you.'

'I asked him to warn the others at Whitechapel and Bermondsey.'

'Perfect! It will require many of us to stop these brutes.'

'And what are they doing exactly?'

'Truthfully, I still do not know. Jack the Ripper and Dracula arrived first. Hyde and Gray joined them less than an hour ago, each with a dead body on their shoulders. They put them in a vault and then went to find the other two in one of the mausoleums located under the great cedar tree. I believe that they are drawing up a strategy. But I am sure of one thing: we must use the fact that they are all together to act. It will be a long time before we get another chance. Now, follow me! And go quietly! They might hear us.'

As I walked beside Sherlock Holmes's ghost I discreetly studied his outfit. Unlike that afternoon, he was wearing a tailored suit, which made him look thinner than normal, beneath a checked coat that fell to his ankles and whose ectoplasmic opalescence concealed its true colour.

For the first time I could observe his face close up. His features seemed to be a skilful combination of those immortalised by Sidney Paget in the *Strand Magazine* and those of Arthur Wontner, whom I had seen a few weeks before at the cinema in London.[14] Under his deerstalker, his gaze was cold and determined, and the tense muscles of his face betrayed his extreme mental strain, entirely preoccupied as he was with successfully completing our mission.

In comparison with the last séance at 221 Baker Street, I observed that my companion was increasingly demonstrating the natural authority that had always been the prerogative of Arthur Conan Doyle's hero. It was clear that, finding himself compelled to investigate an authentic case worthy of his prestige and reputation, Holmes was finally imposing himself and revealing his true nature.

We followed the path for about one hundred yards before arriving at another crossroads. Holmes pointed out a wider avenue on the left with his long, thin, milky-white index finger. In front of us, at the end of the avenue, was a monumental portico flanked by a pair of Greco-Egyptian columns, overrun by brambles and wild vines. It was like being suddenly transported through space and time to the reign of an ancient sovereign worshipping the gods of the dead and hell. Under the portico, an open gate revealed a long open-air view of mortuary crypts.

'This place is called the Egyptian Avenue. Hyde and Gray left the bodies in one of those crypts.'

'Did you have time to check what was inside?'

'No. I remained hidden under the large cedar tree to watch our fellows. I did not want them to escape. As for the contents of those mortuary chambers, I fear the worst, my young friend. Go to the end of the avenue and watch the surrounding area. I will go and have a look.'

I walked along the avenue whose slight dip added to the spookiness of our surroundings. I had the impression, which I have never forgotten, that as I passed through the portico I suddenly entered a sacred dimension where the struggle between the forces of good and evil had been fought for all eternity.

Once at the end of the avenue, the setting was even more disconcerting. The Egyptian Avenue led to another path, this one entirely circular and along which were a series of mausoleums, each more sumptuous than the one before. In the middle was the fixed point around which the rest revolved like the earth on its axis: an immense rotunda containing a number of crypts. At the top of this circular structure, which had a garden in the middle, grew a formidable, majestic cedar tree.

This must be the famous City of the Dead. The number of

tombs was impressive. I hoped that the monsters were still where my companion had left them, otherwise it would not be easy to flush them out.

As Holmes had asked me, I took up position in front of the last crypt on the Egyptian Avenue so as to check if anyone came. During that time the famous detective visited several of the mortuary chambers. When he came back his face was despondent. He put his hand on my arm as if to discourage me from going to see for myself.

'I found where they are hiding their trophies. The bodies can be counted in dozens, piled one on top of the other. The bodies of men, women and children, some drained of their blood, others gashed in several places, others still with limbs removed. It is an unbearable spectacle.'

'Good heavens. So they have changed their tactics and stopped leaving proof of their abominations behind them.'

'Clearly. And where is the best place to hide dead bodies without attracting attention? The City of the Dead, of course, with its many abandoned weed-infested cenotaphs.'

'What should we do, Holmes?'

'I think the best thing is to wait here until Watson and our friends arrive. Hopefully, they will have been intelligent enough to take the same path as us. You see the big mausoleum over there, with a broken cross on top? That's where the monsters were hiding when I came to meet you. They should be there still.'

That was when we heard the muted sound of shuffling behind us. Holmes only just had time to push me against the door of the crypt. He immediately disappeared into the damp, pungent air. Hidden in the doorway, I feverishly waited to see what was going to emerge from the shadows.

As I could not see anything coming, I looked out cautiously and could just make out the phosphorescent form of a fluidic being a dozen yards further along, in front of one of the chambers Holmes had just visited and where he had made his macabre discovery. The figure had opened the crypt and carelessly thrown down the body it had on its back.

At that distance it was difficult for me to see the new arrival distinctly. Eventually he finished his task and turned in my direction. I immediately shrank back against the wooden door, gasping for breath, my heart beating wildly.

The phantom went past without seeing me and continued along the circular avenue. I only had time to observe him very quickly but it was enough to identify him immediately: six feet tall with powerful shoulders, his entire face was hidden under several layers of bandages, large black glasses and a clown's nose.

'Who was that aberration?' asked Sherlock Holmes, reappearing at my side when any danger of being spotted had passed.

'Jack Griffin!' I replied. 'Better known as the Invisible Man.'[15]

'That's all we need!'

'In H. G. Wells's novel, his power makes him slide progressively into murderous madness and in the end all he wants is to spread his reign of terror. He does deserve his place among the great monsters created by the Victorian imagina—'

The end of my sentence dried up in my mouth. Voices could

be heard in the circular avenue and among them I recognised those of James, Dryden and Kirkby. A furious yell followed, which made me fear the worst.

A few yards beyond the mausoleum where the evil spirits were no doubt taking refuge was a stone staircase that was one of the three other entrances to the circular avenue. Unfortunately, that was the one our friends had chosen just as Griffin joined his accomplices and prepared to cross the threshold of the cenotaph.

This was not the time for deliberations. Our friends' lives were at stake. Holmes and I hurried to the circular avenue, which was covered by tongues of creeping fog. At the bottom of the steps, Dr Kirkby was helping Dr Dryden pick himself up with some difficulty from where he had fallen, while James was threatening the psychic presence standing in front of them with his Indian knife. Lady Conan Doyle was at the top of the steps, protected by Dr Watson. Once on his feet, Dr Dryden, shocked, moved back towards the railing to join them.

At that moment, alerted by the noise, the other fluidic figures appeared in the doorway of their cenotaph like a muslin curtain. They were all there: Jack the Ripper who had almost run us through the previous night, Gray, Hyde and Dracula. The features and general appearance of these beings in their extreme plasticity corresponded quite accurately to the image created by the collective imagination. Hyde was absolutely horrible to behold and immediately made all my muscles tense. He had short deformed limbs, giving him a curious gait, together with a protruding lower jaw and the ape-like face of a brute without heart or morals. Dorian Gray looked like a dandy and had the frozen gaze of those for whom detachment and insensitivity have reached such a degree that they no longer belong to the human race. As for Count Dracula, dressed in a dark suit, a white shirt and flannel waistcoat, and a long black silk cape, Bela Lugosi's cinematic interpretation, seen by the world the year before, had manifestly had time to make its indelible mark on the imagination of my contemporaries.

The monsters had not yet seen Holmes and me, and were standing between us and our friends. I drew my kukri knife and brandished it conspicuously as I advanced.

They were cornered. If I could surprise those damnable ectoplasmic creatures before they turned around, busy as they were staring angrily at my companions, I might have time to reach two of them with my dagger. During that time all James and Dr Kirkby had to do was use the element of surprise and strike one each.

But that was to reckon without our phantoms, who were also possibly armed. When they too drew their daggers I saw my friends' look of confusion. Then a noise came from the top of the steps and I guessed from Dr Dryden and Lady Conan Doyle's terrified faces that there was a further complication. Rising up behind them and forcing them up against James and Dr Kirkby were two new spirits to add to the others.

'Blast!' groaned Holmes, who was quick to recognise their faces. 'I should have guessed: Professor Moriarty, the "Napoleon of Crime", and his sinister lieutenant, Colonel Sebastian Moran!'

The detective had spoken too loudly. Mr Hyde, Dorian Gray and Count Dracula immediately turned and glared at us with great hostility, which did not bode well. This time it was all over; they had seen us. But more surprises were to come. On the other side of the circular avenue, coming towards Moriarty and his henchman, were the phosphorescent forms of a number of other phantoms. At their head was an individual with black hair, wearing a light serge suit and a wide-brimmed straw hat, whom I immediately recognised as the ghost of Dr Moreau, the mad doctor created by Wells. James and our friends had no means of escape. Holmes and I were similarly encircled because, with an obscure premonition, I turned my head and saw the spectre of a wonderfully beautiful woman with deep chestnut-brown hair, which fell in heavy curls flecked with silver, coming up behind us, surrounded by an army of grey shadows hovering in the fog.

'Carmilla Karnstein! The female vampire created by Joseph Sheridan Le Fanu!'[16] I exclaimed, instinctively waving the Gurkha knife over my head as if that could frighten the immense fluidic troops who had formed around us.

'Carmilla!' echoed Holmes. 'My word, they're coming from all sides! We must leave or I wouldn't bet on either of us surviving the night!'[17]

That is when Sherlock Holmes did something I will never forget. Grabbing me firmly by the shoulders, after enveloping me in his great milky frame, he whispered in my ear, giving the order to advance and cut through the diabolical line of Jack the Ripper, Hyde, Gray, Griffin and the Count so that we could join the others. Fearing that I had heard him rightly, my heart began to beat faster and a freezing sweat dripped down my spine. I glanced at the creatures in front of me with terror: Dorian Gray and Jack Griffin were provoking us by twirling the blades of their daggers, arrogant, sure of their strength; Jack the Ripper's face was a bottomless void, smoking like a volcano whose simmering violence threatened to drag us into its white darkness; Mr Hyde was sniffing the air like a wild beast ready to pounce; Dracula, his eyes burning into mine, was trying to read my mind to see what we were planning; behind us Carmilla and her troops were only a few yards away and preparing to throw themselves on us. The idea was ridiculous but I had nothing else to suggest and, as Holmes repeated his order with more authority, I let myself be guided like a child taking its first steps, my nerves shaken and my eyes closed. I preferred not to see what my more than certain death would soon look like.

After a few seconds, feeling that we were advancing without encountering any opposition and that we had almost joined our group of friends, I opened my eyes again and looked at Holmes stupidly. His face was shining with a gentle light under the pale moon.

'Make a circle, back to back!' he ordered in a stentorian voice when we were all reunited. 'Move closer together and hold the blade of your knives on the outside. That way they will not touch you.'

'But they'll escape!' cried James, watching the phantoms who were walking round us and regrouping in front of the cenotaph.

'Do not fear. I know how to make them disappear – for ever!'

Did our enemies understand that there was nothing they could do to harm us? After a few minutes, having wisely adopted the position Sherlock Holmes had ordered, we saw the group of monsters withdraw, some of them disappearing into thin air, others scattering down the Egyptian Avenue.

'How the devil did you get past them, Holmes?' asked Dr Dryden who, although in great pain with his arm, had lost none of his sangfroid. 'They divided as you passed like the Red Sea before Moses!'

At first Holmes did not reply. He had moved to one side and his face was terribly serious.

At the top of the steps the moon came out from behind the clouds; at our feet the fog began to disperse gradually.

James looked at me questioningly. I replied with a shrug of the shoulders to show that I did not know any more than him.

I noticed that for a moment Watson was tempted to join his friend but changed his mind. Instead, Sherlock Holmes solemnly turned in our direction.

'Alas!' he said. 'For a long time I did not want to admit that all these tragic events were connected to my presence here. But you were right, Dr Kirkby. My appearance at and moving in to 221 Baker Street for the last few months has created a tremendous reservoir of psychic energy to which these creatures came to strengthen themselves. I have no choice: only by agreeing to return to my invisible world will I be able to prevent other tragedies from happening. To answer your question, Dr Dryden, that is why the monsters let me through before. They could have thrown themselves on me and destroyed me but they did nothing. They need me. If I disappear, they disappear too.'

Holmes paused and paced up and down in front of the cenotaph, which had served as a hideout for our enemies. Finally, he turned to us again, looking sombrely at us one after the other, and then went up to Lady Conan Doyle.

'I would like it to be you, Lady Conan Doyle, who asks me. I will bow to such a request from your lips and will never be tempted to come back. I give you my word.'

Lady Conan Doyle looked at us, confused, but then seemed to understand the tragic nature of that moment. Her face tense, she walked the last few steps which separated her from Holmes and, in a voice broken by emotion, said those words which, after all these years, still resonate in my ears.

'I implore you from the bottom of my heart: leave this place as quickly as possible and never come back – never! I will be eternally grateful, as will Sir Arthur, I am sure. As for your fame, all of us here, and especially myself, will work relentlessly to ensure that it never dies.'

The spirit knelt, took Lady Conan Doyle's hand and delicately brought it to his lips. From our respective places, we distinctly thought we heard the sound of a kiss.

'It is time, Watson!' announced Holmes, getting up. 'Ah, my dear friend! What better place than a cemetery to rejoin the kingdom of the dead, don't you agree?'

Watson, clearly satisfied with the decision his eternal companion had made, kissed Lady Conan Doyle's hand in turn and then stood by the detective's side.

They both moved to the steps by which James and the others had arrived. After a couple of paces, they turned and raised their hands slightly. Then the phosphorescent figures of Dr Watson and Sherlock Holmes disappeared from our astonished gaze for ever.

EPILOGUE

THE ghost of Sherlock Holmes kept his promise. After Dr Dryden had assured himself on several occasions that the first-floor sitting room was no longer plagued by its uninvited guest, Major Hipwood and his wife returned to 221 Baker Street and were never again disturbed by unexplained phenomena.[18]

In the following weeks James and I scrupulously checked the press in the morning and evening but we found nothing that bore any resemblance to the macabre string of murders that had been the talk of the town. The theory formulated by Sherlock Holmes's ghost at Highgate Cemetery had proved to be correct: his return to his own world had brought about the liquidation of the psychic entities that symbolised Victorian Evil. At the very least, it had made them sufficiently powerless to keep them on the other side without means of escape. To use Arthur Conan Doyle's words, *the lodgers had returned to their boxes*. It was to be hoped that they would stay there.

After those incredible three days, I happily resumed my lazy habits of reading and writing. James was keen to make the most of a few days' perfect tranquillity and became slightly intoxicated with football and swimming.

On 18 August, a month and a half after it had all happened, I received a letter from Canada, or more precisely from Halifax in Nova Scotia. I recognised my father's handwriting. As well as news of my brothers and sisters, and more personal considerations on which I will not dwell, his letter congratulated me on the part I had played in the happy outcome of the case of the Baker Street Phantom. At the time I was very surprised that my father was aware of these events; after leaving Major Hipwood's house on Sunday 26 June, it had clearly been agreed among the various participants that we would not speak about what had happened, at least initially. However, as I read on, the mystery became clear. Our dear Dr Dryden had rushed to publish a precise account of the facts in the magazine *Light* where he was full of praise for the perceptiveness of Andrew Singleton, the son of his Canadian colleague, and the courage of James Trelawney. Although the popular press had fortunately not repeated this information (readers of the spiritualist press remain limited generally and non-believers would no doubt have considered Dr Dryden's solution to be a ridiculous hoax), spiritualists the world over had been informed in a trice. I did not blame the good doctor for his indiscretion and wagging tongue; the publicity from that first triumph in the spiritualist world was very useful in the case of the Furrowed Walnut Tree which occurred a few weeks later. Similarly, I am somewhat indebted to Dr John Dryden for the success *in extremis* of the Belgian Judas affair and, to a lesser extent, the case of the Strange Mr Heller that I undertook alone, just after the death of my faithful associate.

Needless to say, my father was delighted to learn of my changed point of view concerning the ideas he had always supported and was looking forward to holding lively discussions with me on the subject soon. Alas, life did not give us that pleasure.

Francis E. Singleton enclosed a surprising article with his letter, published on 26 July in the *Toronto Daily News*. It described a series of séances organised by Dr Hamilton at his home in Winnipeg. According to the article, and the extracts of notes reproduced by the journalist, it was clear that the spirit of Arthur Conan Doyle had tried to communicate with the group throughout the spring and that, during the last séance organised on 27 June (the day after our case ended), Dr Hamilton had managed to photograph the face of the British writer, smiling and serene, in a stream of ectoplasm flowing from the nose of the medium Mary Marshall.

The account of that last meeting particularly caught my attention.

According to Dr Hamilton, it was above all the extremely strong determination of the spirit guides Walter and Katie which led to the successful teleplasm of Sir Arthur Conan Doyle during the now famous séance of 27 June.

On the photographic plate a great ectoplasmic mass about twelve inches long can clearly be seen flowing from the medium's nose to the bottom of the mouth. The part around the moustached face is relatively thick and shapeless while the bottom part is very thin.

Before the picture was taken, Walter-Dawn had predicted that 'a lady' would be seen, amongst other things. This is an obvious reference to one of the four faces on the plate. Among them, the face in the top part of the plasma, the man with the moustache, is undoubtedly Arthur Conan Doyle. But who did the profile of the lady Walter had mentioned belong to? And the small bloated face? (Dr Hamilton claims that he recognises a photograph of the preacher C. H. Spurgeon taken when he was young.) And the death's head?

As to the meaning of what strongly resembles an illustrated allegory, here is the explanation given by Dr Hamilton: on the left, the outline of the young woman could represent immature humanity looking at the skull on the right, a symbol of death. In the centre, the preacher could symbolise the source of spiritual nourishment. In the top part, Conan Doyle's smiling face could represent the validity of his teachings on the reality of life after death and could manifest his joy at enlightening the world about that great truth.

Of course, those of us who had been involved in every part of that incredible affair could understand the meaning of the rebus composed by Arthur Conan Doyle for the living. If the skull did indeed represent death, it was violent death: the Grim Reaper, who, over those few months, had set his heart on numerous victims, including poor Anna Leigh – and not the preacher Spurgeon! – whose bruised face I recognised at once in the ectoplasmic mass, in between the death's head and the outline of the woman. As for the lady, there was no doubt that it was Lady Conan Doyle (indeed, she confirmed it when I showed her the article sent by my father) when she was still the young, beautiful Jean Leckie, the woman who would arouse an all-consuming passion within the heart of the successful writer. Finally, at the top of this enigmatic triangle, the exhausted face of Sir Arthur proved, if proof were required, that his spirit had been watching us anxiously from the other side and that he thanked us for concluding such an audacious mission.

In some respects, that picture confirmed the views held by Lady Conan Doyle during her first visit to us at Montague Street. It did appear that, although Sir Arthur's spirit had been unable to communicate with his wife or any of the other players in the drama for a reason which was still unknown to us, he had repeatedly tried to send messages through Dr Thomas Glendenning Hamilton, a friend who shared his faith in spiritualism and who had acquired significant experience in contacting psychic entities over the years.

Why had his attempts to communicate with us directly not been successful? No one could say for now. A number of mysteries still surround communication with spirits. However, it is probable that it was Arthur Conan Doyle who was behind his wife's premonition of incredible tragedy, encouraging her indirectly to come and consult us on Friday 24 June. And, after all, there was nothing to show that his contribution was limited to those painstaking attempts. Examining it more closely, who knows what other signs of his occult activity might be detected behind many episodes in our adventure?

I hastened to tell Lady Conan Doyle this joyous news which further strengthened the bonds of close friendship that had grown up between us during our investigation.

In the months which followed, James and I saw Lady Conan Doyle and Dr Dryden on several occasions. They had been reconciled and we participated in spiritualist séances organised at the magnificent house of Windlesham. At some of those meetings I was able to contact my dear mother and, as Blanche had predicted, witness the materialisation of her spirit, which was a moment of intense joy each time. What is more, outside my visits to Windlesham, I continued to have news of Leonor Singleton thanks to Lady Conan Doyle's automatic writing skills. Up until her death in 1940, I often received, when I was least expecting it, a charming letter from Sir Arthur's widow together with a few sheets of paper written in a state of trance in which my dear mother gave me advice through Jean Leckie. Advice which proved to be very precious during the Silver Ashtray case and which is why I am still here today.

As for the enigmatic Ashley Kirkby . . . well! Readers have not heard the last of him . . .

A.S., 8 December

NOTE TO THE READER

*T*HE *Baker Street Phantom* is a work of fiction. Although several characters are real historical figures and many of the events described did indeed take place (Sir Arthur Conan Doyle's trips to Canada, the renumbering of Baker Street, etc.) this story is purely the product of my imagination.

The idea for this novel came from the long hours I spent examining the incredible photograph known as Conan Doyle's Return which, two years after his death, revealed the writer's face in a stream of ectoplasm during a séance organised by Dr Hamilton. To view the photograph, I invite the reader to consult the American Photography Museum's website (http://www.photography-museum.com/doylefalg.html).

Studying the history of the photograph and how it was obtained, I discovered the considerable amount of material (photographic as well as literary) that Thomas G. Hamilton had accumulated on the subject of presumed contacts with the other side until his death in 1935. In particular, *Intention and Survival* (a book published posthumously by Macmillan in Toronto thanks to the efforts of his widow, Lillian, and her son, James D. Hamilton) contains a number of extremely powerful passages. I wanted to pay homage to the memory of that surprising man by making the results of the séances organised between March and June 1932 the background to my story.

The *Toronto Daily News* never described the meetings of the Hamilton group, either in the 26 July edition or any other, and the beginning of the article at the start of the novel is entirely invented. However, the rest of the article is strongly inspired by Chapter VIII of *Intention and Survival* where accounts of various communications with the spirit of Sir Arthur are described. The sections in italics are extracts from those accounts.

I should clarify that during the séance on 17 April the message from Conan Doyle's spirit, obtained by automatic writing, was not 'The lodger has left his box. He absolutely must return! He must! A.C.D.' but as follows: 'I am watching your progress. Your methods are different from mine, but perhaps they are better. I will put my picture through if your control will consent. Splendid work! Splendid! Good mediums! My life's work! Carry on! Keep the banner waving. Good night. A.C.D.'

I therefore advise curious readers to read that book, available on the International Survivalist Society website (www.survivalafterdeath.org), or to consult the archives of the University of Manitoba which contain a vast number of documents relating to the experiments carried out by Dr Hamilton from the early 1920s to 1935.

NOTES

1. Black Hawk is the name of another spirit guide. The term 'control' refers to a psychic entity, which can control the séance. (Note from the Editor of the *Toronto Daily News*)

2. Holmes described the case as the third of his career. 'When I first came up to London I had rooms in Montague Street, just round the corner from the British Museum.' According to this description, Sherlock Holmes's rooms were at the top of Montague Street; Singleton and Trelawney's lodgings were further down the road, opposite Russell Square. (Publisher's note)

3. This law dated back to 1733 and its original aim was to combat witchcraft and vagrancy. During the nineteenth and beginning of the twentieth century it was used by the English authorities to imprison a large number of mediums, treating veritable charlatans in the same way as individuals working in good faith, in order to prevent abuses of trust. The meeting Lady Conan Doyle mentions ended in failure for the spiritualist delegation. (Publisher's note)

4. In the past, the numbering of streets with odd and even numbers was not systematic. Before the early 1920s, anyone walking down Baker Street from the Portman Square end on the right-hand side would pass No. 1, No. 2 and so on until No. 42 at the junction with Paddington Street. Crossing the road and returning in the other direction, the pedestrian would pass No. 44 (although why 44 and not 43 no one knows!) and all numbers until 85.

    When Baker Street was extended, the more usual system of numbering was adopted with the odd numbers on the left-hand side of the street and even numbers on the right. So No. 85 became No. 1 and No.1 became No. 2. (Publisher's note)

5. The Society for Psychical Research. Created in 1882 by the philosopher and poet F. W. Myers, it is one of the oldest and most dynamic spiritualist societies in Great Britain. Many well-known figures have been members. (Publisher's note)

6. From 1922 a spirit known as Pheneas, who, in his own words, had been an intrepid Arab warrior in life, began to speak through her by means of automatic writing. The Conan Doyles put all Pheneas's prophecies together in a book and published it in 1927 under the title *Pheneas Speaks*. (Publisher's note)

7. This was putting it mildly. At the beginning of 1930 Arthur Conan Doyle had resigned sensationally from the SPR, just as, two years earlier, he had left the London Spiritualist Alliance of which he had been chairman. He judged these organisations to be too rigid. In reality, the members of these societies were not too upset as the writer's prophecies had proved to be false and his stance disarmingly credulous. (Publisher's note)

8. Conan Doyle's resolutely apocalyptical and messianic beliefs at the end of his life were distasteful to the traditional spiritualist organisations, which were trying to promote their theories within a rigorous and scientific institutional framework. (Publisher's note)

9. Elizabeth Stride, 45, was killed on 30 September 1888. Jack the Ripper was interrupted while he mutilated her. The same night Catherine Eddowes, 46, was also murdered. He removed one of her kidneys and most of her uterus. The memoirs referred to by the author could be *Lost London: The Memoirs of an East End Detective*, written by the former sergeant Benjamin Leeson and published in London by Stanley Paul in 1900 or thereabouts. (Publisher's note)

10. The bookshop was also a small publishing house. Some of Arthur Conan Doyle's last spiritualist books, which had been rejected by other publishers, were published under that name. (Publisher's note)

11. Mary Louise Conan Doyle was the daughter of Arthur Conan Doyle and Louise Hawkins, the author's first wife. A second child was born from that marriage, a boy called Kingsley who died of Spanish flu on the Western Front in 1918. (Publisher's note)

12. In the absence of more details, it is difficult to know which stories he is talking about. However, it is interesting to note that, unlike almost all the other Holmes adventures, four short stories are not narrated in the first person by Dr Watson: 'His Last Bow' (1917) and 'The Adventure of the Mazarin Stone' (1921) are told in the third person; 'The Adventure of the Blanched Soldier' (1926) and 'The Adventure of the Lion's Mane' (1926) are narrated by Holmes himself. The latter two short stories were among the last to be published. (Publisher's note)

13. If one follows Dr Kirkby's theory, according to which psychic beings are energised by the imagination of the living, it would have sent shivers down our spines to recall that, a few months beforehand, Tod Browning's *Dracula* had been released in cinemas across the world. It was a considerable success, as was Rouben Mamoulian's *Dr Jekyll and Mr Hyde*. It should be noted that ten years beforehand the two characters had already appeared in screen adaptations: the first thanks to Friedrich Wilhelm Murnau with Max Schreck in the role of Nosferatu, the second thanks to John Stuart Robertson, with John Barrymore. But at that time neither Dr Kirkby nor myself nor anyone else had dared study the truth in all its terrible dimensions. (Author's note)

14. Sidney Paget illustrated thirty-eight Sherlock Holmes stories from 1891 to 1904 and provided more than three hundred drawings. He was the one who dressed Sherlock Holmes in his famous deerstalker, an accessory which cannot be found in the writing of Conan Doyle. Arthur Wontner played the role five times between 1932 and 1936. (Publisher's note)

15. At the time of this adventure, twelve of the most brilliant writers at Universal Studios in Hollywood were in the process of working on the screen adaptation of Wells's novel. R. C. Sherriff's script won the day and filming of *The Invisible Man*, directed by James Whale with Claude Rains in the role of Griffin, began at the end of 1932. (Publisher's note)

16. The film version of *The Island of Dr Moreau*, adapted from Wells's novel and produced by Erle C. Kenton, was released in January 1933. But the script and choice of Charles Laughton for the main role were already established by the end of spring 1932. Paramount began shooting in October. In March 1932 the film *Vampyr or the Strange Adventure of*

David Gray by Carl Theodor Dreyer was released, adapted from the book *Carmilla* by Le Fanu. (Publisher's note)

17. I discussed this issue subsequently with Dr Kirkby on many occasions and we reached agreement on the point that from 1931 to 1932 the concentration of cinema adaptations of these evil characters was the main reason behind the power of those ectoplasmic manifestations that spring. Furthermore, the actors playing these Victorian heroes undeniably served as models for their fluidic manifestations. (Author's note)

18. The Hipwoods did not live at the prestigious address for long. At the beginning of 1933 they decided to move permanently to their house in Devon. In 1935 several houses were demolished, including theirs, and a large office building was built in its place bearing the numbers 215–229. As Dr Dryden knew several members of the local council, it is not impossible that he supported this project which did away with 221 Baker Street for good. (Author's note)

Singleton and Trelawney Investigate

THE DREAM KILLER OF PARIS

by

Fabrice Bourland

(Translated by Morag Young)

Enter the world of supernatural crime investigation . . .

In the autumn of 1934 a Channel crossing to France takes a paranormal turn for private detective, Andrew Singleton, when he sees an extraordinary mirage and has an encounter with a lady in white.

On arrival in Paris he is quickly drawn into a very unusual murder investigation in which the victim appears to have died of fright in his sleep.

Who caused this death and how? And could there be some connection to Singleton's experience on the Channel? In a city alive with surrealism and metaphysical research, Singleton and his partner James Trelawney set off on the trail of a criminal mastermind, whose evil methods and motives will prove bizarre beyond their wildest imaginings.

ISBN 978-1-906040-32-1

£7.99

www.gallicbooks.com